THE MASTER MUST DIE

Gyron de London, a powerful industrialist of the year 2190, receives a letter warning him of his doom on the 30th March, three weeks hence. Despite his precautions — being sealed in a guarded, radiation-proof cube — he dies on the specified day, as forecast! When scientific investigator Adam Quirke is called to investigate, he discovers that de London had been the victim of a highly scientific murder — but who was the murderer, and how was this apparently impossible crime committed?

JOHN RUSSELL FEARN

THE MASTER MUST DIE

Complete and Unabridged

LINFORD
Leicester

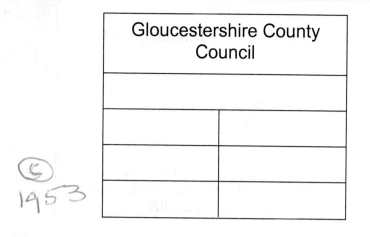

Gloucestershire County
Council

British Library CIP Data

Fearn, John Russell, *1908 – 1960*
  The master must die.—Large print ed.—
Linford mystery library
1. Detective and mystery stories
2. Large type books
I. Title
823.9'12 [F]

ISBN 978–1–84617–753–8

Published by
F. A. Thorpe (Publishing)
Anstey, Leicestershire

Set by Words & Graphics Ltd.
Anstey, Leicestershire
Printed and bound in Great Britain by
T. J. International Ltd., Padstow, Cornwall

This book is printed on acid-free paper

1

Death foretold

Everybody called Gyron de London the 'Master'. Technically, he was not the ruler of 2190 London, nor of the British Federation — but he was certainly the power behind the Government of the time. Gyron of London, to give him his title in more correct parlance, was one of the most powerful industrialists to ever be spewed up from the financial and industrial deeps. He had behind him an unsavoury record — the age-old story of a climb to eminence over the bodies of less sagacious and less ruthless people . . .

In 2190, at the age of sixty, Gyron de London was at the height of his power — feared, respected, hated. Yes, most certainly hated, chiefly by the little, forgotten people who had in some way felt the impress of his pitliless personality.

Forgotten people? Yes — as far as De London was concerned. But there was one, somewhere, who had not forgotten.

To De London, March 9th in this favoured year was no different from any other day. He breakfasted, was helicoptered to the towering edifice which was the root base of his mighty industrial empire, and the elevator whirled him silently up eighty-two flights to the summit where lay his private office. As usual everybody salaamed and smiled frozenly as he swept through the general reception centre. He grunted perfunctory 'good mornings' and went on his way, a juggernaut released for another day's merciless crushing.

'Pig,' murmured an under-clerk, putting away a file.

'Beast,' whispered a girl teenager, who had long since summed up her employer from afar.

The elders said little though they thought much. They watched De London's progress across the broad areas to his office and wished he were at the devil. Amongst the women clerks were conjectures as to how his wife and son tolerated him.

The private office door slammed. The shadow on the glass panel showed that De London, industrial master of the Federation was removing his hat and coat.

'Good morning, Mr. De London . . . ' The voice was a woman's — a chilly, 'keep-your-distance' voice — and it said the same words at the same time every day except weekends.

'Morning,' De London growled, and turned to look at Miss Turner, his First Secretary. She held down her job for two reasons: one because she was inhumanly efficient, and two because she knew a thing or two about her boss's private escapades. To dismiss her would be yelling out for trouble.

'Anything important?' De London questioned, settling at the desk.

'Apparently not, sir. Usual routine mail and messages.'

'Hmmph.'

Miss Turner waited in respectful silence, studying the man who had been her employer for sixteen grinding, pitiless

3

years. He still did not look much older than when she, a girl in her teens, had brightly applied for an office post — and thereafter gone down the hill of acid spinsterhood. Now she was thirty-four, angular, youth entirely lost, her face cynical and hard-drawn.

Yet the man at the desk could have passed for an early fifty instead of being ten years older. He was bull-necked, red-faced, a hard breather and a hard liver. Grey eyes, veiny on the whites, a bulbous nose, and the most vicious mouth which ever disgraced a human face.

'If Consolidateds don't dance to my tune soon, Miss Turner, there's going to be trouble,' he said briefly, studying one of the letters. 'They have the damned nerve to haggle over my proposition — Write them. Tell them my last statement was final and unalterable.'

'Yes, Mr. De London.'

'Also . . . ' More letter perusal. 'Also, contact Amalgamated Copper and up the price by a tenth. That'll teach 'em to waste my time.'

'You think that wise, sir? After all, the market — '

'I am the market, Miss Turner. Do as you're told! As for Steel and Iron, you can write and tell them to — '

De London stopped in mid-sentence. Miss Turner, who had been making brief notes, glanced up in surprise. De London had never been known to stop halfway in anything, even in a sentence.

'I'll be damned,' he said finally, staring at a message. 'Of all the infernal, blasted audacity!'

'Sir?'

'Look at this!' And Miss Turner found a note thrust into her bony hand. She read it, and her expression did not change. It was made up of letters from odd newspapers to form into an under-standable message. It said briefly:

TODAY IS MARCH 9th, 2190. TODAY YOU ARE THE MASTER OF THE INDUSTRIAL FEDERATION. IN THREE WEEKS, ON MARCH 30th, 2190, YOU WILL BE DEAD — NOT FROM NATURAL CAUSES BUT

BECAUSE A SWORN ENEMY HAS DECIDED IT. YOU CANNOT AVOID IT.

THE MASTER MUST DIE!

'Obviously a joke,' Miss Turner said, handing the note back.

'Obviously. I suppose a man in my position must expect a little occasional tomfoolery like this.' De London's brows knitted for a moment as he looked through the note once again; then he tossed it on one side and continued ploughing through his correspondence. When he had dealt with it he gave Miss Turner a sharp look.

'Do you think anybody in the office staff could have put that ridiculous note together?'

The woman shrugged. 'They're any of them capable of it, sir. You are hardly — er — popular with the staff.'

'Lot of damned rubbish,' De London muttered; then he waved a beefy hand upon which diamonds sprouted like warts. 'All right, that's all. If Shelly calls tell him to go to blazes, with my compliments.'

'Very good, sir.'

Miss Turner went out with the silence of a wraith and for several moments De London sat musing, his podgy hand pulling at his lower lip. He could not decide why, but that infernal note had disturbed him. Could there be anything more absurd? He, who was absolutely shockproof, was disturbed!

Muttering to himself, he got to his feet and wandered to the mighty window that looked out over London. From it there was a view that De London always appreciated. He could see the vast metropolis in which he had been born, and which he had conquered. It made his vast power seem transiently all the greater . . . Grim-faced he looked into the canyons of streets, then up to the morning sky, where aircraft and space machines followed their appointed courses —

'In three weeks you will be dead, and not from natural causes . . . '

'Damn!' De London snapped, pulling himself together. 'This is no way for Gyron de London to behave!'

He turned back to the desk, and then suddenly a thought occurred to him. From where had the message been sent? He should have looked for that sooner instead of thinking of the note itself. Seating himself again he dived his hand into the wastepaper canister and finally retrieved the envelope which he had cast away.

He saw now that the envelope had been addressed in the normal way, in a backwardly-sloped hand. The superscription was of the orthodox kind: Gyron de London, Esq., London, Earth. Earth? De London gave a start and then glanced at the stamp on the envelope. It was a Martian stamp, embossed with the crest of the Martian ruling faction. The letter had been physically sent from Mars then, by old-fashioned mail.

De London began to grin, feeling relieved at the same time. He had a host of near-at-hand enemies on Earth and was not scared of any of them. Since this reactionary was evidently on Mars — either a disgruntled Martian or an outcast Earthman — there was nothing to worry about. The space lanes could be watched: anybody suspicious could be arrested. Nothing to worry about . . .

Just the same, De London did not throw the message away. He put it in his wallet along with the envelope and then did his best to banish the whole thing from his mind. Banish it? He might as well have tried to stop the sun moving. The memory of the note kept obtruding every time he allowed himself a few seconds to think outside his business demands.

'If it worries you so much, sir,' Miss Turner said, catching him out wool-gathering, 'why don't you tell the police? They'll very soon deal with the matter.'

De London smiled scornfully. 'The police! I never yet found them any use in a crisis. Too much wind and too little action. Besides, it would be the devil of a come-down for me, the most powerful man in the country, to have to admit I am scared by a child's prank.'

'With all due respect, sir, I would submit that this is hardly the work of a child. Harmless, yes, but devised by somebody quite malignant. And candidly, I think you wrong the police quite a deal. Whilst I was on Mars recently for my vacation I lost my suitcase and — '

'On Mars? Vacation?' De London looked up sharply. 'When?'

'After Christmas, sir — ' Miss Turner looked surprised. 'Surely you remember? You gave me extension of time.'

'Yes — Yes, so I did. I'd forgotten. I had overlooked that you had a Martian vacation.' De London made a sudden effort and pulled himself together. 'Well, that's all I require at the moment, Miss Turner. I think I'll leave early today. I've a lot to catch up on at home. My son is bringing his fiancée to see me, I think.'

'Oh.' The First Secretary smiled without warmth. Since romance had passed her by, she could hardly enter into the spirit of the thing. She picked up the signed letters and departed to her own quarters. After she had gone De London sat looking at the closed office door.

'Been to Mars, has she? And recently? Now I wonder . . . I'm not fool enough to think but what that sterile has-been has nothing but animosity for me. Her idea of a joke perhaps? Make me squirm a bit? If so, heaven help her.'

It was a possibility, of course, that the First Secretary was playing games, but somehow De London could not credit it. Miss Turner hated him — he well knew that — but he did not credit her with imagination enough to launch a one-woman campaign against him.

'No — remote from possibility,' he decided. 'Nonetheless the Martian coincidence might be checked. Have to think about it.'

He pressed the intercom button and in a moment was speaking to Rogers, his chauffeur and general factotum. When not transporting his boss in either the car or helicopter Rogers spent his time doing odd jobs about the De London estate — as at this moment. But at any second the radiophone on his wrist could bring him to attention.

'Yes, sir?' he asked respectfully.

'Bring the helicopter, Rogers. I'm leaving earlier than usual. Fifteen minutes deadline.'

'Yes, sir.' Rogers switched off and made a sour face. If any man hated his employer, that man was Rogers. For ten years he had stood the big man's oral bludgeoning and come up for more. There was only one reason: he liked the pay and he also liked one of the maids on the domestic staff. He hoped that one day he might claim her and then thumb his nose at De London and all his works.

Rogers got on the move. He deserted the work he was doing in the grounds under the surveillance of the head gardener and headed for the helicopter garage. As he went he turned a matter over in his mind. That morning he had received an extraordinary message, made up of clipped letters from a newspaper. It directly affected both him and 'his employer. Should he mention it, or let the old so-and-so wallow in ignorance?

Rogers was still thinking it out as he flew the helicopter over the enormous metropolis in the late afternoon sunshine. Well under the stipulated fifteen minutes brought him to the roof of the De London Edifice, and he went to seek his master and found him in his private office.

'You've kept me waiting,' De London said brusquely.

'Sorry, sir. The fifteen minutes is only just up.'

'I'm aware of it. You could have been quicker ... Take me to Metropolitan Police Headquarters. I've a matter to attend to.'

'Very good, sir.' Rogers held the office door open and his employer swept past him and through the main reception area. There were brief murmurings of farewell from the office staff, of which De London took not the least notice. Rogers followed him up, arriving in time to hold open the rear door of the helicopter beyond which was De London's sealed, private cabin.

'Been to Mars recently, Rogers?' De London paused in the act of entering his cabin to aim the question.

'Not recently, sir.' Rogers studied the unpleasant, florid face and veiny eyes. 'If you recall, sir, you asked me to forego my vacation this year for extra pay. Couldn't spare me, you said.'

'Did I? I must have been crazy. All right — Police Headquarters, and hurry it up.'

De London finished his half-bent entry into his cabin and settled himself, but Rogers did not immediately close the door. He stood thinking, until he realised his employer was glaring at him.

'How the hell much longer are you going to be, man? Get that door shut!'

'Yes, sir. First, though, I think there is something you ought to know. Your deciding to visit Police Headquarters brings it into my mind.' Rogers fumbled in his uniform and produced a letter with a torn envelope. 'I received it this morning, sir. I didn't mention it earlier because I wanted to think about it. I — er — suppose it's a joke.'

De London snatched the envelope and pulled out the paper from within it. His mouth set hard he read:

YOU ARE ROGERS, FACTOTUM AND MUG TO THE 'MASTER'. THE MASTER MUST DIE — AND IN THREE WEEKS FROM TODAY HE

WILL. NOBODY WILL EVER DIS-
COVER HOW. YOU WILL THEN BE
FREE OF HIS DOMINATION. ON
MARCH 30th. SOMETIME BEFORE
MIDNIGHT HE WILL TERMINATE
THE EVIL CLIMBING TO POWER
THAT HE SO ADORES.

He looked at the envelope and noted
the Martian mail stamp. From the look of
things the newspaper letters had been cut
out by the person who had sent the other
communication. A pair of curved nail
scissors had been used in each case.

'You believe this?' De London snapped
suddenly.

Rogers' wooden face did not move a
muscle. 'No, sir, I don't. A joke, I
suppose.'

'Why don't you add 'unfortunately' and
speak the truth?' The industrialist gave a
harsh grin. 'I'm not going to be
murdered, Rogers, believe me! You might
as well know now: I had a note similar to
this one this morning, threatening me
directly. Hence my visit to Police
Headquarters . . . I'll keep this one of

yours to add to my own.'

'Just as you wish, sir. I'm glad I allowed my better judgment to prevail in this matter. I'll get on the move right away.'

The cabin door closed and Rogers swung up into his own little glass-sided compartment. In a matter of ten minutes he was bringing the helicopter down again on the roof of Police Headquarters — once Scotland Yard — and after opening up his master's cabin he sat down to await his return.

De London was not a man to mince matters. He came right to the point as he faced the Commissioner for Metropolitan and Interplanetary Crime across his huge polished desk.

'Read these,' the industrialist ordered, and tossed the two messages onto the desk.

The Commissioner obeyed. He only had his job because De London willed it, so vast was the tycoon's influence.

'Seems like a joke,' the Commissioner said finally, raising his eyes.

'I'm not interested in what it seems to be, Commissioner. My life is being threatened, and whether it is a joke or not I want action and prompt, ruthless justice. No man — or woman — can do this sort of thing to me and expect to get away with it.'

'No, Mr. De London, of course not. Er — have you any particular enemy that you know of who might be domiciled, or connected with, Mars?'

'I've enemies by the thousand. No big man can avoid 'em. But I can't name anybody specific ... ' De London considered, his paw pulling at his lower lip. 'Or can I? There's a bit of a mystery about my First Secretary. She had a vacation recently on Mars and she hates me like all hell. She could have spent her time dolling up two messages like this and then have left them for the delayed mail so they wouldn't arrive until many weeks after her return to Earth.'

'And do you think she might carry out the threat implied in these notes?'

The industrialist grinned. 'Not she! She hasn't the brains. Secretarial work is about her limit. Her only reason for this bit of handiwork would be the wish to see me squirm.'

'Which you are doing?' The Commissioner was coldly polite. 'You must be, sir, to go to the length of coming here?'

'I'm the best judge of whether I'm squirming or not. Let's see, who else is there? Rogers, maybe. He's my chauffeur, pilot, and general washer-up. Bit of inscrutable sort of devil and likes me about as much as prussic acid. A stunt like this wouldn't be beyond him. Might even be able to put the threat into effect.'

'What makes you think that, sir?'

'Well, he's pretty ingenious: I know that much. Maybe he gets it from his father. His old man was a physical scientist, and I used quite a number of his inventions. Maybe the son has similar gifts. Serves me right for taking pity on the son and giving him a job when his father died. He was left pretty well on his uppers. He was his father's assistant.'

The Commissioner nodded, thinking. 'All very interesting. Mr. De London, but a trifle vague as a basis upon which we can get to work. I've made a note, anyhow. Anybody else you can think of?'

'No, I don't — ' De London stopped, his eyes sharpening, Abruptly he banged his fist down on the desk. 'Why the blazes didn't it occur to me before?' he demanded. 'Orwena Tirgard!'

The Commissioner looked respectfully interrogative.

'Owena Tirgard!' De London insisted. 'Yes, of course! She is my son's fiancée. Martian girl, part Earthian on her father's side. Half-breed, of course. I can't stand her at any price and she knows it! Now, I just wonder . . . '

'Certainly a more positive lead than any so far,' the Commissioner agreed. 'And from what I know of Martians, whether pure-bred or half-breed, they're a mysterious lot of folks. Originally Earth-born, of course. A group of scientists and private entrepreneurs who colonized Mars at the end of the last century, creating their own protected environment on that dead world, and proclaiming themselves independent from Earth. Brilliant, secretive, highly educated. I'd rather like to meet your son's fiancée and form some conclusion.'

'That's easily fixed. He's bringing her home this very day — much to my disgust. Something important he has to say regarding the pair of them. The wife's all for it — but I'm not. And if I can smash the romance I shall.'

The Commissioner smiled faintly and wondered if De London ever got tired of smashing things — lives, careers and markets.

'If you could invite me to your home, just as a friend,' he suggested, 'I might get a lead.'

'Very well.' De London got to his feet. 'Be there tonight at eight o'clock and I'll fix everything. There's a sort of celebration been fixed by that stupid wife of mine because of Harry's return home. Dammit, he's only been away six months . . . Right! Eight it is, and see you're not late. I've no time for unpunctual people.'

De London departed and spent his time thinking as he was flown home by the impassive Rogers. Once within the residence the tycoon discovered that the lounge had already been commandeered by a host of friends — or at any rate, acquaintances — of his wife. He took one look at them, grunted uncivilly, and was about to leave when his wife caught up with him.

'Just a minute, Guy.' She caught at his sleeve. 'I want a word with you.'

'Later,' he growled, making to move on.

'Now!' Eleanor de London insisted, and as usual she had her way. It was not that she dominated: she simply had the sublime gift of handling the raging beast in his lair. So De London sat down on the edge of the thronging, laughing guests and waited.

'It's about Harry,' his wife explained, settling beside him.

'Can't it wait? I want to freshen up and change before getting entangled with this mob.'

'He's not just bringing Owena to meet us as his fiancée, Guy. She's his wife.'

For once De London looked almost stupid. His wife's blue eyes were earnest.

'Isn't it wonderful?' she smiled. 'Harry has married at last! Now perhaps he'll settle down and do something useful instead of living on what you allow him.'

'Married?' De London repeated slowly. 'Married? To that little Martian upstart? That half-breed!'

'Ssssh! Remember the guests.'

'Blast the guests!' De London surged to his feet. 'What the devil does he mean by going behind my back and marrying this creature? I've only seen her once so far and what I did see I didn't like.'

The assembly paused in their murmurings to each other, and looked in surprise towards their hosts. Mrs. de London gave an uncomfortable smile and edged her husband towards the doorway. In the quiet of the hall she gave him a frank look.

'If you must blow up, Guy, please do it in private. Come into the library.'

De London growled something under his breath and lumbered after his wife's still slender, tripping figure. In the library he slammed the door and waited, glaring at her.

'I won't stand for it,' he declared flatly. 'Not only am I not consulted before this marriage, but — '

'Why should you be consulted? Harry's twenty-seven and perfectly entitled to please himself.'

'To a certain extent, yes, but he is the son of Gyron de London the most powerful man in the British Federation. For that reason his machinations in matrimony should first have been submitted to me . . . '

'They were. Did he not bring Owena to meet us? The dear, sweet girl that she is.'

'He did not say he intended to marry her. That was left as so much assumption. The son of De London marries a Martian half-breed! Great God, what next?'

Eleanor de London looked troubled. 'I don't understand your attitude, Guy; really I don't. Owena is the daughter of a very high-born Englishman and an equally high-born Martian woman. After all, her mother is one of the Nardins of the Controlesque, descended from one of the original families who colonized Mars. She is one of the highest women advisers to the Martian controlling body — equivalent of an aide-de-camp to a ruling monarch.'

'Monarch?' De London's voice dripped with acid contempt. 'None of those blasted Earth colonists were of royal blood: they only proclaimed themselves as such when they settled on Mars and severed ties with Earth! She's nothing but a half-breed. I as good as told Harry — and Owena — I didn't approve of their association, which was one reason why they took themselves off to Mars, I suppose. I even refused Harry his last pay cheque when he wrote for it. I did that to show my displeasure.'

'Then you'll have to get pleased again,' Eleanor de London smiled. 'They're married, and that's that.'

'Perhaps. When I don't like a thing, Eleanor, I smash it. I can do it with people and markets. I can do it with a marriage. I will not have my son entangled with a Martian woman. No Martian is to be trusted. Having renounced all ties with Earth, they are jealous of our planet's resources, and are constantly scheming against us.'

Eleanor de London's brows knitted for a moment; and at length she sighed.

'Please don't make a scene, Guy, when Harry and Owena arrive. It'll make such a bad impression on the guests.'

'Oh, damn the guests! I didn't invite 'em, anyway. Bunch of parasites, the lot of 'em. They wouldn't be here if they didn't feel sure of free food and drink . . . I'm telling you straight, Eleanor, when Harry and Owena arrive I'll raise hell! Now I suppose I'd better be thinking about getting ready for the evening. No blasted peace no matter what!'

Upon which De London stormed out of the library. For him to be bad-tempered was not unusual — but to be so bad-tempered was a surprise, even to his wife who knew him so well. But then, she was unaware of the note he had received and the effect it had had upon him. He would probably have been the first to deny that the warnings had in any way affected his equanimity, but it was so just the same.

An hour later Harry and Owena arrived and from that moment Eleanor de London was involved in manifold strategies to keep the smiling pair amidst the guests, where she hoped they would be safe from her overbearing husband. For as long as possible she kept the news of their arrival from him, but it eventually leaked out through one of the manservants.

Down came De London to discover how much he had missed — and there was a curious pause amongst the high spirits of the guests as the industrialist came into the great lounge. Everybody looked at him — grim-faced, freshly-shaven, resplendent in faultlessly-cut evening clothes.

'Hello, dad!' Harry de London broke the tension and came forward with his hand extended in greeting. He was a tall, good-looking young man, the kind almost any girl could have found attractive.

'So you've got back?' The tycoon ignored the hand. 'Without saying a word to me you get married. Am I to understand that I am a nonentity in your calculations?'

Harry flushed a little. 'Nothing of the sort, dad. I married because I wanted to, and it wouldn't have made the slightest difference whether you'd permitted it or not.'

'So it seems.' The industrialist brushed forward until he was facing Owena. She was a slender girl of uncertain age, entirely normal in physical contour, since Martians and Earthlings had few dissimilarities in physique, thanks to the artificial gravity devices with which their enclosed settlements were equipped, which gave the Martian colonists an Earth-normal gravity.

The only unusual thing about her that stamped her quasi-Martian origin was her eyes. They were big, innocent, with over-large olive green pupils. They made her look inordinately fascinating when contrasted with her ivory-white skin.

'I suppose,' De London asked her bluntly, 'that you inveigled my son into this marriage? Maybe as revenge because last time I saw you I made it clear I did not approve of you?'

'Guy, for heaven's sake!' Eleanor de London was waving her hands about helplessly.

'Well?' De London barked, and the half-breed girl studied him inscrutably and then smiled.

'Harry and I married because we love each other,' she replied simply. 'Is that so hard to understand?'

'It will be to him, yes!' Harry snapped, coming forward. 'Dad hasn't the remotest conception what love is. Ask anybody who works for him, who has been stamped on by him! The Master speaks — and somebody dies!'

The industrialist turned slowly and surveyed the faces of the guests. Some were looking awe-struck; others disgusted.

'I see no reason why any of you ladies and gentlemen should continue to take up room in my household,' he said bluntly. 'Certainly I have no wish to detain you.'

Eleanor made a sound rather like a groan, and for the next ten minutes she was engaged in the unenviable task of having to apologise and say farewell to the scandalised guests as they took their departure. Throughout the exodus De

London stood watching them stonily, Harry glaring at him. The only one who appeared entirely unmoved was Owena. She sat beside one of the occasional tables sipping at a rare essence.

'The air seems sweeter now,' De London said at last when the door had closed on the last guests. 'Let it be understood by you two that that is the measure of my intolerance towards your union. I warn you I shall do everything in my power to break your marriage — and I do not have to embellish the fact that my power is far-reaching.'

Harry took an angry step forward. For an instant he looked as though he would strike his father across the face then Owena's gentle hand on his arm detained him.

'Don't, Harry — not on my account anyway. It isn't you whom your father hates so much. It's me. Am I not right, Mr. De London?'

'Exactly right! You are a Martian, Owena, and in my experience not one of your blasted race is to be trusted. You owe no allegiance to Earth, only to your own enclosed artificial world. My son would never have married you had you not seduced him in some way!'

'She did no such thing!' Harry stormed. 'Owena's a decent, sweet girl, and I'm proud to have her as my wife. By what damned right do you dare say such things about her?'

'I dare,' De London sneered, 'because I am your father — because I am much more experienced than you — and because I know what subtlety the Martians possess! Why should I bless your union when my very life has been threatened by somebody who is at present resident — or was resident — on Mars?'

'Your — your life has been threatened?' Eleanor came forward in alarm. 'When, Guy? You never told me!'

'No reason why I should. I'd have had no sympathy anyway. I'm not going into details. I'm merely saying I do not approve of this marriage, and both of you will oblige me by leaving this house — and staying away! If, later, I legally smash your union I will consider then, Harry, whether I'll permit you to return.'

Harry laughed shortly. 'Thanks for the insult, dad. We'll go all right — and gladly. You needn't think because you've stopped my pay-cheque that I can't make a living for myself. I already have a job in the city. I fixed it definitely before coming on here for the 'reception'.'

'I see.' The industrialist shrugged. 'I'd thank you to use some other name than your own. I don't fancy my son being linked with the ordinary masses. Bad for prestige.'

'I'm sticking to my name, and my wife,' Harry replied. 'Let's be on our way, Owena.'

'Where will you be staying?' Eleanor asked quickly catching at them as they passed by her.

'We have our eye on a nice apartment,' Owena smiled. 'When we get the address fixed we'll let you know.'

'That will be quite unnecessary,' De London told her and the half-Martian girl gave him a steady look.

'For you, perhaps, but not for Mrs. de London. I'm sorry you hate me so, because it is quite ill-founded.'

De London smiled bitterly. 'Ill-founded? I wonder? My life has been threatened by somebody on Mars, as I've already said. I'd stake a good deal that the 'somebody' is you.'

'That's a pretty rotten thing to add to the barrage of insults you've already fired!' Harry blazed.

'Or even you might have sent it,' De London added.

Harry hesitated, obviously about to ask for full details of the mysterious threat his father had received, but Owena stopped him. She nodded her dark-haired head silently towards the door and then moved away with easy grace. There was a certain finality about the way that door closed. It hurt Eleanor de London quite a lot — but not her husband. Entirely satisfied with the situation he settled down to read a stock market report until it should be time for dinner.

At eight o'clock the Commissioner of Police arrived — and left again, a much bewildered man. His instructions were to pursue Harry de London and his wife and examine their activities in detail. If there was the least sign that either of them had sent the threatening letters — De London clenched a massive fist at the thought. He would smash, and smash and smash!

2

Death delivered

After the explosion within his domestic sphere an abysmal calm settled on Gyron de London. He had admitted to himself that the real reason for his unusual outburst could be traced to nerves, and the nerves to the threats he had received. It was necessary therefore to cut the thought of the notes right out of his consciousness. He must behave as though they had never existed.

He might possibly have succeeded in this intention, had it not been for the fact that upon reaching his office the following morning he found a further message awaiting him, bearing the customary Martian mail stamp.

Miss Turner made it plain what she was thinking though she did not actually comment. De London ripped open the envelope and read the message through quickly. It said:

MARCH 30th. THIS IS IN CASE YOU MAY HAVE THOUGHT THAT THE EARLIER MESSAGE WAS A JOKE. IT WAS NOT, AS IN THREE WEEKS YOU WILL HAVE AMPLE OPPORTUNITY TO DISCOVER. THE MASTER MUST DIE!

'Another?' Miss Turner asked quietly, and her employer gave her a bleak look.

'Damned well obvious, isn't it? I can't imagine what the Commissioner of Police is doing. It's time he had got this absurd business in hand — Put me through to him.'

Miss Turner switched on the visiphone and within seconds De London was looking at the Commissioner's face on the scanning screen. Miss Turner hovered, until she met her employer's steely eyes.

'You can get out,' he said, and waited until she had done so; then he gave his attention to the 'phone. 'I've had a fresh threat this morning, Commissioner. Whoever it is seems to mean it. How far have you got in solving the business?'

'Nowhere, sir. I'm not a magician, and these things take time.'

'I don't want excuses, Commissioner, I want results. If I don't get them there'll be trouble — What happened in regard to my son and his half-breed wife? Did you locate them?'

'Yes, sir, I did. I engaged them in conversation in the lounge of the Trident Hotel. In the best unofficial way I could I tried to learn something from them, but was unsuccessful.'

'And that was the best you could do?' De London barked.

'I have not the power to do anything more, sir. I have nothing specific to hang on to either of them — '

'Then find something. I'm becoming more sure than ever that that wife of my son is at the back of it. She's half-Martian, she hates me, and she's damned clever behind her pose of youthful innocence. Pin her down somehow. Break her!'

'Yes, sir,' the Commissioner promised, patiently. 'And I also have our inter-planetary men checking up on the other leads you gave me.'

De London muttered something uncivil and switched off. As he sat thinking Miss Turner came in again.

'Your chauffeur, Rogers, wishes to see you, sir,' she announced.

'He what?' De London started. 'What the devil's he doing here? He ought to be back at the estate doing some work — All right, show the fool in.'

In a moment or two Rogers entered, peaked uniform cap in his hand. De London fixed him with an arctic stare.

'Well?' he demanded.

The chauffeur came forward, no expression on his wooden face. From his uniform he took an envelope, the flap of which was torn, and put it on the desk. It had the Martian mail stamp.

'I thought I'd better come back right away with this, sir. It had arrived by the second mail when I returned from bringing you here. It's another . . . warning.'

Smouldering to himself the industrialist whipped the message from the envelope and scowled at it:

YOU HAVE NOT LONG TO WAIT FOR FREEDOM. YOUR MASTER WILL BE DEAD AS PROMISED BY MIDNIGHT ON MARCH 30th. THIS IS IN CASE MY EARLIER COMMUNICATION FAILED TO REACH YOU. THE MASTER MUST DIE!

'I do not understand,' De London said slowly, 'why this blasted upstart always has to communicate with you at the same time as communicating with me. What business is it of yours?'

'I don't know, sir. I'm as puzzled as you are.'

'I wonder . . . ' De London's veiny eyes slitted. 'This upstart keeps speaking of you getting your 'freedom'. What kind of stories have you been spreading abroad about me? Been making me out to be a tyrant?'

'Certainly not, sir. I know my station.'

'It's to be hoped you do. If you ever

talk out of turn, Rogers, I'll smash you into small pieces. You'll never get another job anywhere on this planet. You'll finish up as a space machine rocketman, maybe. There's nothing lower than that.'

Rogers was silent, not as much as a flicker crossing his carven visage.

'I'll keep this note,' De London decided, after a pause. 'The Commissioner is handling things so he'll need this one along with mine.'

'Very good, sir. I take it, from what you say, that you have had a second warning?'

'I have: this morning. Not so much a second warning as a reminder of yesterday's. By God, if only I could get my hands on the swine who's at the back of this . . . '

Rogers hesitated, then: 'It is hardly my place to point an accusing finger at a possible suspect, sir,' he apologised, 'but did you ever think of . . . your son's wife?'

'Owena Tirgard, that used to be? Before the marriage?'

'Yes, sir. Mr. Harry's wife. I just happened to think — she being of half-Martian origin, and then the things she said about you on the way home yesterday — '

'Eh? What's that?' De London's eyes sharpened. 'Said about me?'

'Yes, sir. She must have known that I couldn't help but hear her because it was when I picked her and Mr. Harry up at the spaceport in the helicopter to bring them home — '

'Be damned to that! What did she say?'

'I can't remember the exact words, sir, but it was to the effect that you deserved blotting out — that was her expression — for the way you'd stopped Mr. Harry's money. Your son remonstrated with her when he realised I must be listening, but she only repeated her statement and said that one day, and perhaps soon, you'd get all that was coming to you.'

'And then?'

'She said no more, sir. I drove her and Mr. Harry home in the helicopter after that.'

The industrialist nodded slowly, his lips tight; then looked at the chauffeur across the desk.

'Normally, Rogers, I wouldn't dream of discussing private issues, like this with you — but circumstances alter cases. You have received notes as well as me, so you know all the facts. I am suspicious of Mrs. de London junior, yes — so much so I told her last evening to get out of my house, and my son too. I shall see to it that the Commissioner hears of this latest development. It strengthens the case against my son's wife very considerably.'

'Yes, sir.' Rogers half turned to go; then turned back. 'Am I permitted to make a suggestion, sir? Concerning your safety, I mean?'

'Suggest all you like. I don't have to accept it.'

'Well, sir, if this Martian young lady is at the back of this, she can very probably carry out her threat on the thirtieth of March. In fact she'll be far more able to carry it out than any Earth person. The Martians are extremely clever scientists.'

'I know that, you damned fool.'

'Well, sir, that being so, this woman might find ways and means of killing you which would escape detection by Earth experts. Your one way of defeating anything like that would be to put yourself in an impregnable position on March thirtieth. It seems pretty clear nothing will happen before then, so why don't you fix yourself so that during the twenty-four hours from midnight on the twenty-ninth to midnight on the thirtieth nothing can assail you?'

De London straightened up a little. 'Go on talking Rogers. Maybe you're not such a wooden-faced bonehead as I've always thought.'

'No, sir, maybe not. My father was a scientist, remember, and I have a similar bent myself. I was just thinking, if this woman uses radiations or ultrasonics, or something like that, to kill you they'd be invisible and untraceable. Their effects might even be put down to heart failure. If, though, you put yourself in a radiation-proof chamber of tungsten steel, on the lines of a bank strong-room, and had the place surrounded by armed guards throughout the twenty-four hours, nothing could kill you.'

'Perhaps,' De London mused, 'you

really have an idea there, Rogers.'

'Thank you, sir.'

'The only thing which puzzles me is, why are you so anxious to save me from being killed? You don't love me any more than anybody else does. What's behind it?'

Rogers shrugged. 'I wasn't thinking of you particularly, sir, but the scientific angle. If a Martian is planning to kill you, it will be a great triumph for Earth's foresight to defeat the intention. At least, that's how I look at it.'

'I see. All right, I'll think it over. Now get back to work.'

'Very good, sir.' Rogers turned and departed silently, leaving De London in deep thought. Finally he nodded to himself and pressed the intercom.

'Miss Turner? Send Dr. Matthews in to me right away.'

'Yes, sir.'

Dr. Matthews was head of the scientific division in the vast De London enterprises and had his quarters elsewhere in this enormous edifice. After a lapse of ten minutes he arrived — a tall, composed man with a beaked nose and deep-set eyes.

''Morning, sir.' He hated De London as much as everybody else. 'Anything wrong?'

'Nothing beyond the fact that my life has been threatened, and possibly by a Martian who may use ultra-scientific methods to dispose of me.'

'Indeed?' Matthews' brows rose as he was motioned to a chair. 'I'm sorry to hear that.'

'No you're not, so don't waste time. I've just been thinking of a possible way to circumvent what appears to be a very genuine threat on my life. Suppose radiations were used, or ultrasonic vibra-tions: can insulation against them be provided?'

'Very simply, sir — yes. The most penetrative radiation that can be used is in the cosmic ray order and in these days Lead J2 is the answer to that. It's a new type of lead composite, one-foot thickness of which will block all radiation, including cosmic. We use it on the space ships, as you're aware.'

'I've heard of it,' De London admitted, though in truth he had not. He had never heard of anything much outside the jingle of money. 'I take it, then, that if a chamber like a strong room were built entirely of tungsten steel, with a lining of Lead J2, nothing could get through it?'

'Nothing, sir.' Matthews shook his head with profound emphasis. 'We know the range of nearly all Martians' wavelengths and radiations and they certainly would not get through that!'

De London gave a grim smile. 'That suits me fine. I want you to get engineers to work immediately to convert half of this office into the kind of strong, insulated room I have outlined. No windows, no anything — just an absolutely hollow cube with a small airlock for entry. Not even a ventilator. Put in an air-conditioning plant, same as are used on spaceships.'

'Very well, sir.' It was not Matthews' job to question his employer's orders. 'I'll put the outline to our chief draughtsman and have him draw a preliminary plan for your approval.'

'Do that,' De London nodded, and Matthews promptly left the office.

By late afternoon, by which time De London was in a much happier frame of mind, the sketch was finished. Matthews himself brought it and laid it on the desk. It was not a complicated layout by any means. There was the steel cube with its hollow interior, the inside area measuring twelve feet by twelve by twelve. Furniture consisted of a wooden table and a type of camp bed. Nothing more.

'Design's all right,' De London said finally, 'but I shan't have any furniture. If I sit anywhere it'll be on a rubber cushion which I can inflate myself.'

Matthews looked surprised. 'But, sir, for twenty-four hours! You must have something on which to sleep, and a table at which to eat.'

'In that twenty-four hours, Matthews, I'll be too damned uneasy to sleep. As for food, sandwiches can be brought by one of the guards, or something. Maybe not even that in case there is a chance to poison them. In regard to the furniture, it might leak out that I'm using it in the safety room and something might be concealed in the table or chairs to kill me. No! Just myself, the clothes I have on at that time, and a rubber cushion. That is the limit.'

'Very well, sir. You wish me to put this in hand for construction?'

'Make it tomorrow. I have somebody else yet who ought to see this plan — just to vet it.'

'As you wish, sir. I await your pleasure . . . ' and the scientist went back to his quarters.

The 'somebody else' to whom De London had referred was, of course, Rogers. In normal circumstances De London would never have dreamed of taking the chauffeur-cum-handyman into his confidence but in this case he might be able to suggest even more ideas for defeating any lethal enterprise.

So he was shown the sketch before De London departed from the office in the helicopter. Rogers arrived in the normal way at 5.30 to announce to his employer that the helicopter awaited him.

'Apparently, sir, this will do all that is

required,' he agreed, after considering the sketch carefully. 'I notice one point has been neglected — an essential one.'

'Oh? What's that?' De London looked surprised.

'I assume, sir, you do not wish to sit in the dark for twenty-four hours? When that airlock has been sealed from the inside by you there will be total darkness within the cube and no provision has been made for electric light.'

'I'll be damned! Surprising how the vital spots get missed. I'll have that attended to. Anything else?'

'Not that I observe, sir. If I might be permitted to think it over — '

'Yes, do that. Tomorrow morning let me know — '

'Oh, Mr. de London . . . '

The tycoon turned quickly. Miss Turner had been standing some little distance away, waiting for the conversation to finish. Now she came forward, as angular and unbeautiful as ever.

'Well?' De London snapped, annoyed that she had had a chance to see what was going on.

'That letter to Amalgamated Copper, sir. Is it to go electronically or ordinary mail?'

'Electronic — for speed. Anything else?'

'No, sir. I just wanted to be sure.'

De London compressed his lips as the secretary went back to her own quarters, then he picked up the sketch and thrust it into his pocket. Rogers held the door open for him and then followed up to the 'plane park on the roof.

And by the next morning, since no new ideas seemed to have dawned on Rogers, the sketch was handed over to Matthews with instructions to have the engineers go to work immediately. There was no trouble about this: when the Master gave an order — and one of such urgency — no effort was spared to carry it out. And, since De London had given the deadline as two weeks, engineers worked night and day in order that there could be no delay.

With intense inner satisfaction the tycoon saw the steel room taking shape. The walls were a foot thick with radiation-proof materials, and utterly impenetrable. The electric light was of the standard variety, the wires passing through a tungsten steel tube in the roof of the cube, thereafter being connected to the normal supply wire.

The door was put on last, every bit as massive and difficult to hinge as the door of a strong room, but by the time the engineers had finished it swung with absolute smoothness and latched with easy silence.

During this constructional period the only two intruders to behold the strong room were Miss Turner — who could not help but see it anyway — and Rogers. Since he knew all about it in any case there was no point in hiding it from him. When, at rare intervals a business associate entered the tycoon's private office he was told that the cube was a new type of strong room for the storage of valuable documents.

So the days passed. There came no more warnings, but nonetheless De London kept his eye on the calendar, and he also selected eight highly trusted men to act as guards during the twenty-four hour period of approaching 'confinement'. By March 28th the strong room was complete. Nothing remained but for the tycoon to step inside it and shut himself in. Even the bolts of the hermetically sealing door were operated from the inside.

Strong man though he was, however, and despite the fact that he pooh-poohed all the threat that hung around his head, De London was nevertheless human enough to suffer from strain. By the 28th his nerves were in rags, so much so he began to wonder if death were, perhaps, going to come by natural causes and that the unknown had foreseen such a possibility.

On the 28th De London visited a specialist for a complete overhaul, fully fearing the worst from the diagnosis.

'Been having extra business worries recently, London?' the specialist asked, when he had finished probing with his instruments.

'Not exactly.' The tycoon hesitated. 'Business is more or less satisfactory.

What worries I have had have been domestic. My son has made an unfavourable marriage for one thing . . . '

'Mmmm. It's something more than that. How about smoking?'

'No more than the usual ten cigars a day.'

'I feel,' the specialist said, shrugging, 'that you are not being altogether frank with me, London. However, that's up to you. As to your condition, you need rest. Severe overstrain of nerves and heart. Driving yourself too hard.'

'To keep up with my various commitments I have to, man. I don't quite understand why this overstrain should suddenly develop. I thought such a condition came in gradually.'

'As a rule it does, which is why I am seeking the cause. Some sudden shock to the system has brought it about. You know in your heart what that 'something' is, but prefer not to tell me. That's it, isn't it?'

De London evaded the question and instead asked one himself.

'How bad am I? Am I likely to . . . die?'

'One day, yes — same as all of us. As you are now you'll last many years yet, provided you take things a little more easily. That's all I can tell you. There's a new restorative medicine recently been produced which will do you a world of good. I'll let you have the prescription before you go. Give me your word you will take it three times a day at ten, two and six o'clock without fail. If you don't you may terminate your life quicker than I believe.'

The specialist was one man whom even De London could not brush aside, so he gave his promise and had the prescription made up the moment he returned home. Thereafter he delegated the task of being reminded about the times for the medicine to the ever-watchful Rogers.

So to March 29th, a day of tense expectancies and medicine dosages at the correct times. No further warning. Nothing except the grim inevitability of the calendar.

March 30th. Miss Turner, cool and efficient and, somehow — unless De London imagined it in his disturbed state of mind — she seemed to be secretly gloating. Rogers came at ten in the morning and two in the afternoon with the inevitable medicine and found his employer making a desperate effort to keep a grip on himself.

Time and again during the day De London went into the strong room and looked about him. Everything was normal. The walls, ceiling and floor were all radiation-proof steel. No windows. No ventilator. In one corner stood the standard air-conditioning equipment, of the exact type used on all space machines. Nothing suspicious there. Overhead, hanging from the steel tubing, was the electric light, extinguished at the moment of course. Yes, everything here was normal.

It was in mid-afternoon that Miss Turner came in with an announcement that made De London's face set harshly.

'Your son and his wife to see you, sir.'

'Tell them I'm busy. I never felt less in the mood to see anybody — let alone them.'

'Very well, sir — ' Miss Turner turned

away to carry out her instructions, but before she could do so the office door opened wider and Harry de London came in, the quiet figure of Owena immediately behind him.

'Just in case you decide against seeing us, dad,' Harry explained dryly, coming forward — and at that De London gave a head-jerk of dismissal to the secretary.

The door closed. De London sat back in his swivel chair, biting on his cigar.

'Well, sit down,' he invited gruffly. 'What do you two want? I was under the impression you'd walked out for good to make your own lives.'

'That,' Harry admitted, settling Owena, 'was the intention. But things are tougher than I'd expected. I haven't managed to hold down that job I got.'

'So now you come bleating to me for help, eh?' De London grinned harshly. 'I can give you the answer right now, Harry — you'll not get a cent, or even a word of sympathy, until you throw out this half-breed wife of yours.'

'I expected that,' Harry said bitterly.

'Then why the hell did you come here?

Let me remind you, too, that I'm busy. The sooner you both leave the better I'll like it.'

Owena's large eyes looked at the magnate steadily for a moment and then turned to Harry.

'You'll have to do it, Harry,' she said, in her low, gentle voice. 'No other course.'

'Afraid you're right, Owena.' Harry looked at his iron-faced father. 'It concerns the affair of Interplanetary Debentures, dad.'

'What about 'em? That matter's years old.'

'Six years, to be exact. I happen to be the only other person in the world — outside Owena, who knows as well — who can prove that you milked the public of multi-millions on that deal and got away with it. You may remember that, six years ago, I did considerable secretarial work at home for you. I have kept confidence with you all that time — as a secretary should.'

'Well?' De London barked.

'Just this,' Harry replied simply. 'I'm no

longer a secretary, and I'm desperately short of money.'

The tycoon got slowly to his feet. 'Are you daring to threaten me, Harry? Is that it?'

'Harry,' Owena explained, smiling, 'is simply trying to make a business deal. It is surely worth say, half-a-million to you to keep the — er — odour of Interplanetary Debentures from reaching the nostrils of the public?'

De London swung on her, his veiny eyes glittering. 'You put him up to this, you no-account Martian!'

'Yes,' Owena admitted, quite unshaken. 'Harry told me about it some time ago when we were exchanging confidences. It occurred to me that since we need financial backing we must use force since you will not provide it voluntarily.'

'I should have thought,' De London sneered, 'that a husband ought to be able to support his wife without recourse to his father!'

'I would be, but for you!' Harry flamed back. 'I lost my job because it leaked out that I'm the son of the Master. I used another name, as you asked, but it didn't do me any good. When the truth came out I was asked to leave. And why? Because you are the most hated man in the city, dad, and any relative of yours is plain poison.'

'So,' Owena added, shrugging, 'it deflects the responsibility for our maintenance to you, Mr. de London. I'm sure the deal is a fair one. Five hundred thousand in return for silence upon a scandal which could crack your empire from top to bottom.'

'Blackmail,' De London whispered, clenching his fists. 'No more than I might expect from a filthy Martian.'

Silence. Harry clenched his fists and his face reddened. De London stood scowling and thinking. Owena's big eyes moved from the magnate's sullen, vicious face to the strong room and its wide-open airlock. She gave a peculiar inward smile.

'All right,' De London snapped finally. 'You have me in a corner and I have to comply. Frankly, Harry, I don't believe that you would put such a blackmailing threat into action, but I can't trust this wife of yours. Five hundred thousand it is — and where is my guarantee you will be satisfied with that?'

'You have only our word,' Owena said; then she gave a gentle laugh. 'How does it feel, Mr. de London, to be in the position of some of your victims? I realise now why you relish the feeling that you can crush, and crush, and crush — '

De London stared at her, his mouth working. He knew he could expect no pity from this woman who was half-Martian and half-Earthian. Though she had seemed to accept his earlier insults lightly she had evidently set herself out to find a method of hitting back — and in a business life such as De London had lived there was plenty to work upon. Now she had struck she had done so with shattering force. It was quite plain, even to De London, that Harry was nothing more than the instrument of Owena's will.

De London swung, jamming his cigar back between his teeth. He returned to his swivel chair and dragged out his personal cheque book from the desk.

Whilst he scribbled he noticed out of the corner of his eye that Harry and the girl drifted over to the strong room and peered inside it. Then they entered and vanished from view.

De London finished writing the cheque and waited, fuming. In a moment or two Harry and Owena reappeared.

'Quite a solid job, Mr. de London,' Owena commented, still with that baffling smile. 'It wouldn't be for storing your more — er — doubtful documents in, would it?'

'Nothing to do with either of you what it's for. Take this cheque and get out!'

Harry took it, and Owena examined it. They both nodded and then without another word left the office and quietly closed the door.

'That I should have a son like that,' De London whispered. 'Lets that damned woman bend him round her little finger. Be different if she had me to deal with — Now what?' he demanded, as Miss Turner came in.

'There are six men here, sir. They say you asked them to report for duty by four this afternoon.'

'Men?' De London struggled to get things into focus. 'Oh, yes! My body-guard! Send them in.'

The secretary departed and presently the six entered. They were all of them six-footers, in the uniform of the city police, and heavily armed. Every man thoroughly to be relied upon. De London had made absolutely sure of that.

'Your orders, men, will not be difficult to carry out,' De London said, eyeing them. 'As you are already aware a threat has been made on my life. It may or may not be carried out. At six o'clock this evening I shall enter that strong room yonder and seal it from the inside. Once I have done that two of you will remain in this office, outside the strong room, until I emerge tomorrow morning. Two others will be in the reception office outside, and another two on the main corridor leading to this office suite. That understood?'

The men nodded promptly.

'That's all,' De London said briefly. 'Take up your positions at five-thirty. In the meantime you can pass your time in one of the ante-rooms.'

The men withdrew, and for the rest of the afternoon the tycoon found himself fully engaged in dealing with business matters. It was six o'clock almost before he realised it and the two men who had the task of guarding the exterior of the strong room entered. Miss Turner, picking up the last of the signed letters, glanced at them, then back to De London.

'It's all right,' the magnate said. 'See you in the morning, Miss Turner.'

'I hope so, sir,' she said quietly, giving him a long look — and then she went out.

The tycoon braced himself a little and switched on the intercom. He ordered sandwiches and a drink and then sat back in his chair. The two guards took up a standing position on either side of the open strong room airlock and remained as immovable as sentries.

The sandwiches and tea arrived. De London ate and drank moodily. Many things would perhaps have happened before he had another meal . . . if he had another meal. He got to his feet and absently pulled a cigar from his case, then remembering the air-conditioning apparatus would not stand up to smoking he put the weed back again regretfully.

He had reached the airlock of the strong room when the office door clicked. Rogers came in, as wooden-faced as ever. De London turned and frowned at him.

'Damn it all, Rogers, you of all men should know I'm not returning home tonight. What do you want?'

'Your medicine, sir. Six o'clock. I have my orders.'

The tycoon smiled wryly. 'Of course, the medicine! I'd forgotten it. All right. Let me have it.'

He wandered into the strong room and seated himself on the big cushion on the floor, the only comfort he allowed himself. Rogers crossed to the desk, removed the medicine glass from the desk drawer, and from the phial he had with him he poured out the required measure. This done he went into the strong room, the glass in his hand.

Five minutes later he emerged again, still with the glass in his hand, but this time it was empty.

'I will report in the morning, sir,' he said, standing in the airlock. 'Seven o'clock, as you have ordered.'

'There are times, Rogers, when I wonder if you're not the only friend I've got,' came De London's voice.

'Thank you, sir.' For a moment Rogers' face relaxed into a half-smile, then with a nod to the guards he went on his way.

After a second or two De London appeared in the airlock, grim-faced and sweating.

'This is where I close the hatch,' he said, switching on the solitary electric light. 'I'll come out again tomorrow morning.'

The two men saluted and helped to pull shut the mighty door. They dimly heard the clamps being slammed home, and then there was silence.

Nothing disturbed the peace from there on. The guards remained on duty throughout the still night, guardians of the dark emptiness of the great building.

Seven a.m. came, but there was no sign of the airlock being opened. Rogers arrived, and waited for a while — until 7.30. Then with the guards he tried to make De London hear through the thick walls — without avail.

Engineers were summoned and after two hours the door was burned through far enough to permit entry. One glance was enough for the men who forced their way in. De London lay on the floor, his head on the fat cushion and the remainder of his gross body on the metal floor.

But one thing was plain to see: he was quite, quite dead.

3

Enter Adam Quirke

The death of the Master was fanfared and trumpeted not only throughout the British Federation but throughout the world. Gyron de London, one of the wealthiest men on Earth, had passed away. The announcements said 'peacefully', an inference drawn from the fact that he did not appear to have suffered any pain upon his demise. He was given a colossal funeral, at which all the high-ups and dignitaries attended. A day of mourning was announced throughout the city . . . then the body was removed to the mausoleum, there to lie enshrined and embalmed for all who wished to gaze upon a man who had climbed to power over the shoulders, and bodies, of others.

By the time a week had passed the business world had adjusted itself again. Somehow the air was sweeter without the iron clutch of the Master. True, there was nobody yet with enough dominance to take his place — and certainly Harry de London, who had automatically taken over his father's control as the next-of-kin, was no autocrat. He was too young for one thing, and apparently had far too much of his mother's good nature in him for another.

Then, by degrees, certain people began to look at each other with an unspoken thought, each one remembering the warning that had reached De London before his death. To all intents and purposes he had died naturally — or at any rate without anybody being near him — but had that really been so? The certain people who exchanged these questioning glances with each other were Harry himself, Owena, Rogers and Miss Turner. And it was Miss Turner herself who finally broke down the tension. She asked for, and was granted by her new employer, a special meeting, and here she put forth the one major interrogation:

'Did Mr. de London die of fear because of the warnings he received, or was some outside agency responsible for his end?'

Harry and his wife looked at each other. Owena's pretty face was blank, expressionless, and gave away nothing. Rogers, the chauffeur, waited for the next, his lantern jaw set and his mouth hard.

'I'm only an employee,' he said finally, 'so I can't see that it really signifies whether I'm here or not.'

'It signifies,' Miss Turner told him, 'because you also had warnings at the same time as Mr. de London, therefore you are, so to speak, as suspect as the rest of us.'

'Suspect?' Owena raised her brows. 'Frankly, Miss Turner, I don't like your tone.'

'I'm not apologizing, Mrs. de London.' The secretary gave her a frosty stare. 'I'm thinking of the various legal aspects of my late employer's affairs. For one thing, there's a fortune in insurances tied up in the fact of whether he died from natural causes, somehow committed suicide, or was murdered.'

'Yes,' Harry mused, 'you're right there. I've seen the various papers to which you refer. I was going to let it pass as death from natural causes — or rather syncope, as the doctor put it on his certificate. Do I understand you question that diagnosis?'

'I don't question the diagnosis, but in view of the threats which preceded the death, forecasting it to the very day, I do think that the doctor may have been misled. Death may have been induced somehow.'

'Very well then,' Owena said, 'let us call in the police and have them investigate. For legal reasons if nothing else we must have a proper directive in order to run this business correctly.'

'I did call in the police,' Miss Turner stated, surprisingly. 'Immediately after I knew of Mr. de London's death. The Commissioner himself took charge of the matter and his cleverest experts went to work.'

'And what did they find?' Harry asked.

'Nothing. But on the chance that something emerges from their scientific analyses back at headquarters they ordered that the strong room be closed and sealed until they gave permission for it to be reopened. That is why it is like that now.'

The others glanced towards it — that mighty hollow cube which had been erected to save a millionaire from his last visitor. The airlock was shut and across it were steel wires welded at the ends into the metalwork.

'I rather wondered about that,' Harry admitted, 'but I've had too many other things to do to question it. You took a lot on yourself. Miss Turner.'

The secretary gave another of her arctic glances. 'That is a matter of opinion, sir. Immediately after the death of my employer there was nobody in control here except me and I felt it my duty to contact the police because I knew of the warnings that had been sent. I was glad I did. The Commissioner already knew of them: apparently Mr. de London had been in touch with him.'

'All of which means you believe murder was done?' Rogers asked.

'I believe so — cleverly, subtly, ruthlessly, the victim already softened up by the warnings which had been sent.'

'And yet the police can't find anything,' Harry pointed out. 'Nothing more we can do, is there?'

'There's one thing we can do, if you will grant me permission, and that is consult Adam Quirke.'

There was silence for a moment, then Owena asked:

'Who is Adam Quirke? I'm not very familiar with the names of important Earth people as yet.'

'Quirke,' Harry told her, with a rather whimsical smile, 'is a scientist of unusual attainments. An eccentric, without doubt, but nonetheless brilliant. He acts as a free agent but is at the back of most of the difficult cases handled by the Interplanetary and Metropolitan police.'

'You mean he's a detective?'

'Yes, if one can say that of a man who arrives at his conclusions by the most incredibly complicated scientific reasoning.'

'I still think he should be consulted,' the secretary said. 'It's quite obvious the ordinary police cannot find anything to get their teeth into. Quirke, on the other hand, might. With your permission I'll call on him and see what he can do.'

'Quite all right to me,' Harry responded. 'What do you think, Owena? And you. Rogers?'

'I'm neutral, sir,' Rogers replied. 'If your wife says 'yes' or 'no' I'm outweighed in any case. I prefer not to cast a vote either way.'

'By all means see the genius,' Owena agreed, spreading her hands. 'I've never seen an Earth scientific detective at work: it might prove interesting.'

Miss Turner got to her feet, frigid as a statue. 'With all due respect, Mrs. de London, I feel compelled to point out that the purpose of consulting Mr. Quirke is not to study his methods but to solve once and for all how Mr. de London senior met his death. I believe we owe him that, no matter what our private feelings might be.'

'You are being insolent, Miss Turner,' Owena observed, a glint in her striking eyes.

'I am stating a fact, Mrs. de London. I spent most of my life working for Mr. de

London and I want to be satisfied as to how he met his death. I will go immediately and see if I can get in touch with Mr. Quirke.'

This did not prove very difficult. Adam Quirke lived in a detached house in the city centre, a house ringed by invisible scientific gadgets by which, through screens and microphone pick-ups, he was able to survey any caller and, if necessary, even register their heartbeats and see if fear were prompting the visit. He read no such signs on the instruments trained on the unsuspecting Miss Turner as she rang the front doorbell — so he actuated the switch which made the door swing open mysteriously.

The secretary hesitated, peering into the clean, highly-polished hall, then she jumped violently as an amplified voice boomed forth:

'Welcome, madam! Straight down the hall to the door straight ahead of you marked 'Private'.'

With some trepidation and feeling rather like a nervous heroine in a movie thriller, Miss Turner obeyed the injunction, and the moment she had crossed the compensator photoelectric beam the front door closed silently behind.

'Amazing, to say the least of it,' Miss Turner muttered, and went bravely on her way. Reaching the door marked Private she tapped upon it and immediately a voice invited her to enter.

She pushed the portal wide and hesitated nervously, gazing upon a large laboratory drenched in the odour of chemicals. She was not quite sure whether to turn tail, call, or go forward. Then she caught sight of Adam Quirke himself and stared in almost rude amazement.

Not infrequently she had seen his 3-D photograph in the newspapers and magazines, but she had not gleaned from them the real dimensions of this eccentric scientific investigator — nor indeed anything of his immense geniality. Adam Quirke was a big man, in every sense of the word, with massive shoulders and what seemed to be nearly seven feet of height. Actually he was six feet nine inches and weighed twenty-two stone. Delicate instruments quivered as he lumbered across the laboratory to greet his guest — and Miss Turner, no more than five feet two, gazed up at him with still that astounded expression in her eyes.

'Good morning, madam,' Adam Quirke smiled, extending a vast hand. 'I notice you are somewhat ill-at-ease. I can assure you this laboratory is quite harmless. Oh — my secretary,' he added, as a woman of perhaps twenty-seven, grey-eyed and fair-haired, came into view with a notebook peeping from her overall pocket.

'I — I must confess my breath was rather taken away,' Miss Turner explained, smiling awkwardly.

'To be sure,' Quirke smiled, and waited with immense indulgence whilst his secretary brought up a chair for the visitor.

'Now, madam . . . ' Quirke eased his colossal rear onto the edge of the nearby bench. ' . . . maybe we can get to business. Miss Brayson will take down all

75

the details whilst I listen. I don't know what I'd do without her. She's my right hand, my left hand, my eyes, my guide — everything but my wife.'

'Oh?' Miss Turner looked vaguely questioning.

'I'm married already,' Quirke explained, grinning — then his grin exploded into merriment and the two women had to wait until the storm had passed. Finally Quirke came up for air, wiping his eyes and blowing like a swimmer who has swallowed too much salt water.

'Mr. Quirke is quite a wit,' Miss Brayson explained, cocking dubious grey eyes towards the mountain.

'What would life be without a joke?' Quirke asked, spreading his hands. 'But forgive me, madam, I digress. Your name?'

'I am Violet Turner, formerly First Secretary to the Master — Gyron de London. Now I hold the same position to his son.'

'So?' Quirke waited. He had a very large face, capped by an untidy mane of snow-white hair. His complexion was as pink as a teenage girl's and his eyes a remarkable china blue. It was in these eyes that the real soul of the man seemed to lie. They varied constantly in expression — sometimes merry, sometimes pensive. And Miss Turner had no doubt they could pierce deeply into any wrongdoer if necessary.

'I am assuming,' Miss Turner continued, 'that you are conversant with the details of Mr. de London's recent death — '

'Quite conversant, madam. He died on the exact date predicted by some unknown threatener, despite the fact that he had sealed himself in a tungsten steel cube and had the aforesaid cube surrounded by guards.'

'You are conversant, Mr. Quirke! May I ask how you — ?'

'The Commissioner of Police is a personal friend. He gave me the details — partly, I feel, in the hope that I would extract some valuable suggestion from the hat. I did not do so.'

'Oh! I had rather thought — '

'I haven't a hat,' Quirke explained

solemnly, and Miss Brayson put down her notebook and stifled a yawn whilst the cataclysm of laughter broke forth again. Through it all Miss Turner also waited, her face becoming even sourer than normal.

'Your forgiveness, madam,' Quirke apologised, dabbing his eyes. 'I cannot resist these quips.'

'Since you couldn't help the Commissioner you obviously will not be able to help me,' Miss Turner said acidly. 'I don't think I need take up more of your time, Mr. Quirke.'

'And yet you came here to ask my advice? Madam, you have not given me much opportunity, have you? I gather you wish to ask the same question as the Commissioner. Was De London murdered or did he die naturally?'

'I don't wish to ask that at all because I'm perfectly sure he was murdered. The coincidence of his death on the fatal date just cannot be accepted as natural causes.'

'I agree,' Quirke rumbled, fondling his four chins. 'Please continue, Miss Turner. Getting it down, Molly?' he asked, with a glance at his secretary, and the blonde head nodded briefly.

'Matter of fact, I have nothing more to say, relative to the actual demise of my employer.' Miss Turner looked vaguely surprised at herself. 'I simply came here on impulse, Mr. Quirke, because I have noticed on many occasions that you have solved problems which have had the police baffled.'

'My fame spreads — like my figure,' Quirke smiled. 'I would remind you, though, that only the scientific problem is of interest to me. If you feel that Mr. de London was scientifically murdered — '

'I'm convinced he was.'

'Why?' The blue eyes sharpened to diamond points and Miss Turner felt suddenly warm.

'Because he went to such lengths to protect himself. That cube-room in which he locked himself was specially proofed against all known radiations, including cosmic. Then there were the guards around the cube. Nothing but a scientific method could have killed him.'

'So,' Quirke mused, 'it would seem.

The Commissioner was more cagey than explicit, I'm afraid, fearing perhaps to sound too ignorant for a man in such a responsible position. Well, madam, what do you wish me to do?'

'Examine the problem, if you will. I haven't come of my own initiative. I'm speaking not only for myself but for the new directors of the De London Organisation, and my late employer's chauffeur.'

'May I ask what the chauffeur has to do with it?'

'He received messages at the same time as my employer.'

'Ah, yes!' Quirke held up one sausage of a finger. 'Of course. I recall the Commissioner referring to that . . . Dear me, I must look through the notes I made at the time and bring myself up to date. So I am asked to find out whether De London was murdered or not?'

'You are asked to find out how he was murdered. Nothing will alter my conviction that he was. For legal reasons we must know the facts.'

'I see.' Quirke levered himself from the bench and stood thinking; then his eyes flashed abruptly back to Miss Turner.

'I suppose it is a waste of time to ask if De London had enemies? Manifestly he must have had in his position. And I was one of them.'

'You!' Miss Turner looked shocked.

'I hated the sight of him.' Quirke smiled blandly. 'Without speaking ill of the dead I feel bound to state that Gyron de London was one of the biggest bullies I ever met. However, that will not influence me in trying to discover who had the good sense to kill him — and more important, how he was killed.'

'Everything regarding the cube-room is still exactly as it was when my employer was found. The Commissioner had it sealed pending further enquiry.'

'Good old Commissioner,' Quirke chuckled. 'I happen to know that right now he's counting the increasing grey hairs on his scalp as he tries to fathom what happened to De London. Well, nothing else for it, Molly, but to desert our current investigation and take a look at this new problem.'

'Yes, sir,' Molly Brayson assented, and

folded up her notebook.

Miss Turner got to her feet. Quirke rid himself of the untidy smock he was wearing and replaced it with an immaculate french-grey jacket to match his trousers. His secretary reached down a dustcoat and threw it carelessly about her.

'You have everything necessary, sir?' she asked Quirke as he adjusted his florid bow tie.

'Everything necessary, yes,' he agreed, then rumbling and choking over his obscure joke he lumbered to the door and pulled it open, watching the two women go out ahead of him.

If Miss Turner had expected the gigantic scientist to talk on the De London problem during the short walk to the city's heart she was disappointed. He merely commented on the weather, the kind of food he enjoyed, and the things he abhorred. It left Miss Turner, efficiency-plus, vaguely disturbed in mind. Had she made a mistake in asking this rumbling, chuckling, joke-cracking mountain of flesh to take up the De London mystery?

They arrived at the De London Edifice fifteen minutes later. In the private office Harry and Owena were still present, going over the files, but Rogers had departed to his duties at the estate.

In silence Owena and Harry watched the three enter, their eyes automatically drawn to the immense figure of the scientist, his mane of white hair ruffled more than ever by the wind.

'Mr. Quirke,' Miss Turner introduced, and then motioned to Owena, seated languidly, and Harry, who was standing. 'Mr. and Mrs. de London, junior.'

'Delighted!' Quirke beamed and shook hands, introduced his secretary, and then settled himself in the widest armchair he could find.

'I trust Miss Turner explained the details, Mr. Quirke?' Owena questioned.

'As much as was necessary, madam. I am already fairly conversant with the case ... ' Quirke's blue eyes were glancing to various parts of the office, including the sealed cube-room. 'I have decided to handle the matter, though I do not guarantee success. I do not pretend to be a superman.'

'That's rather a pity,' Harry said. 'I have the feeling it will need one to get to the bottom of this business.'

'Is that a statement or a hope?' Quirke still smiled.

'Eh? A statement, of course! You don't suppose I want the mystery left in mid-air, do you?'

'I don't know. I just wondered, seeing as you are as involved as anybody. Well now, let's see . . . ' Quirke sat thinking for a moment. 'Fortunately the Commissioner gave me a lot of details so that will save wearisome questioning. You saw your father on the day of his death, Mr. de London, did you not?'

'Yes. It was about the middle of the afternoon.'

'Yes. And both of you had a look inside the steel cube there and then emerged again.'

'I never said so!' Harry snapped.

'No — the Commissioner did,' Quirke smiled. 'You stated that fact to him.'

'Well, yes. He wanted every detail, so I told him.'

'Very wise of you. And I am afraid the fact that you and your wife entered that cube-room automatically casts suspicion on you.'

'Rogers examined it, too, and so did I,' Miss Turner put in.

'I am aware of that also. Which makes each one of you open to complete investigation. I thought I'd make that little point quite clear to start with.' Quirke shifted position slightly and breathed heavily. 'There are some details I have not got, so I may as well have them. Why did you visit your father on the fatal day, Mr. de London?'

'Just a business matter,' Owena replied, at which the blue gimlets fixed upon her, even though the smile remained.

'I am sure your husband is capable of answering for himself, madam. We'll try, shall we?'

'It was a business matter, yes,' Harry confirmed. 'Nothing at all relevant to my father's death.'

'We do not all think alike. I'd like you to be more explicit.'

'Well, I — it was simply a matter of

arranging finances.'

'How arranging them? Surely your father was capable of handling such matters without your help, sir?'

'Er . . . ' Harry stopped and cocked an eye on Owena. She was in the midst of delivering a brassy stare from her large eyes, but apparently it was entirely wasted on the urbane Quirke.

'Let me delve a little,' Quirke said, hunching forward and puffing asthmatically. 'You recently returned from a honeymoon visit to Mars, Mr. de London. Naturally your wife came back with you. The marriage did not have the blessing of your father.'

'That is mere assumption,' Harry snapped.

'Not entirely. If the marriage had had your father's blessing every newscast and paper in town would have blared it forth: that was the De London way of doing things. What happened? A complete silence, even though an almost obscure notice mentioned the fact that Mr. de London junior and his delectable half-Martian wife had arrived at the spaceport. From that I infer that your father did not approve.'

'Correct,' Harry sighed, and did not see Owena's bitter look.

'Good!' Quirke clapped his hands together with startling impact. 'Let us go a stage further. If your father did not approve of the marriage he would hardly support it financially. Yet it used to be common gossip in society that he was your sole financial backing. Result, your income probably ceased. For that reason you made an effort to obtain a position but were discharged, when your identity became known.'

'Who says so?' Harry demanded.

'The Press said so. You do not imagine so important a man as the son of De London could involve himself in trying to take an ordinary job — and losing it — without mention, do you?'

'What are you inferring?' Owena asked sharply.

'I hardly need to infer, madam. The cause of your visit to your father, Mr. de London, was money. You needed some and came to the only source you knew of.'

Harry was silent. He had just seen Owena's hard expression, completely transforming her usually pretty face. Adam Quirke sat back again and mopped his face.

'The amount was five hundred thousand, I think,' he remarked at length. 'I rather wish you'd have admitted it instead of keeping silent. I'm prone to strongly suspect the silent type.'

'This is monstrous!' Harry declared. 'You couldn't possibly know the amount —'

'I again refer you to the Commissioner,' Quirke sighed. 'On your father's death murder was suspected by the police. Accordingly all his papers and personal effects were subjected to scrutiny. In his personal cheque-book was a counterfoil for five hundred thousand, made out to you . . . I'm not a magician: I just have a good memory when I can find time to exert it. Did I get the amount right, Molly?'

'Right, A.Q.,' she assented.

'And what,' Owena asked deliberately, 'has all this to do with my father-in-law's death?'

'I dunno, madam. I'm just scraping facts together and trying to get the limelight fixed clearly on each one of you. To my mind the method of murder is not so important as the motive. The Commissioner takes the opposite view. He would probably have pinned you for murder, on suspicion, Mr. de London, had he been able to prove what you'd done. Since he can't, he's stuck . . . '

'I didn't murder him,' Harry growled, 'even though I often felt like doing so.'

'Thank you for admitting that much. Now, five hundred thousand is a very big sum — the kind of sum your father would never have handed out without extremely good reason, particularly since you and he were at loggerheads. Now suppose we have a little get-together on the reason, eh?'

'You cannot force us to speak,' Owena pointed out.

'Very true, madam. I merely ask for co-operation. Whatever the reason it is better I know, otherwise my endeavours to unearth it may cause you considerable embarrassment.'

'It was hush-money,' Harry said bluntly. 'My father perpetrated a swindle some years ago and I knew about it. So did my wife. Being without money I demanded five hundred thousand from my father as the price of silence. He considered it was better to pay than risk scandal.'

'Blackmail, eh?' Adam Quirke shrugged his gigantic shoulders. 'All right: now we know where we are. Illegal though your action may have been I don't propose to do anything about it because I am not even remotely interested . . . What did you do when you went into that cube-room?'

'Merely surveyed,' Owena replied.

'With Mr. de London senior's permission?'

'Never asked him,' Harry said. 'Just curiosity which prompted us. We didn't know precisely what the strong room was for even though a suspicion had crossed our minds.'

'You just looked around — and what did you see?'

'Air conditioning apparatus, a big cushion on the floor and the electric light flex. Nothing more except the walls.'

'Mmmm . . . ' Quirke sat hunched like a baby elephant that has gone to sleep. Miss Brayson, knowing him so well, was quite aware that he was very much awake, and she went on making notes silently.

'And you, Miss Turner?' The blue eyes opened suddenly and pinpointed the secretary. 'You studied the cube-room too, you say? Why?'

'Purely curiosity, same as Mr. and Mrs. de London here. I knew what the room was for, of course, and I urged my employer to have some furniture, even if it was only a camp bed. He wouldn't hear of it. He was afraid some death-dealing device might be placed in the bed fixture itself.'

'Very wise precaution. And I suppose the cushion came from home?'

'Yes. He brought it himself — wouldn't even allow Rogers to carry it. Rogers is the chauffeur and man of all work.'

'Ah, yes. I must have a word or two with our friend later on. Tell me, Miss Turner, what were your relations with your employer?'

'Entirely normal and businesslike. I will admit right now that I respected him, even though I didn't like him. His power and ruthlessness appealed to me.'

'You hated him, you mean?'

Miss Turner reflected. 'I wouldn't say that. I just — Well, I just didn't like him. He used me as secretary for a number of years and never gave me a chance to make use of my youth. One might say, in a sense, that he destroyed me.'

'Which might make it reasonable to you that you should destroy him in return?'

The secretary gave a steady look. 'Yes — but I didn't.'

Adam Quirke struggled to his feet and breathed hard. Then with his hands in his jacket pockets he began to roam around the big office to the accompaniment of heavy vibrations.

'Regarding these messages which Mr. de London received,' he resumed. 'I haven't seen them since the Commissioner has them, but I will make a point of seeing them. I understand they came from Mars. You, Mr. and Mrs. de

London, spent your honeymoon on Mars — and you, Miss Turner, also spent a vacation there?'

'Yes,' Miss Turner said quietly.

'I trust, madam, the significance of your Martian vacation coinciding with the threats from Mars has not escaped you?'

'I'm perfectly aware that I could be tied up with them, as could Mr. and Mrs. de London here — but I deny all responsibility.'

'Quite — but you doubtless felt a sweet sense of pleasure at seeing your employer's reaction when he received them?'

'I gloated inwardly, yes, when I knew what the messages implied. I felt I was getting my own back for years of being browbeaten.'

'Thank you for being so frank.' Quirke turned away abruptly and heaved his huge bulk over to the cube-room. Pausing, he stood looking at it, his head with its bushy white main tilted to one side. Harry and Owena exchanged glances. Molly Brayson closed her notebook and drifted to her chief's side. Miss Turner sat with her eyes downcast, hands limply in her lap.

'I understand,' Quirke said, without turning, 'that engineers had to blast their way through this door to reach the interior?'

'They did,' Harry assented. 'After that the door was put right again and sealed over, as you see it now.'

'Mmmm.' Adam Quirke did not waste any more time. He seized the wires lying across the door, and pulled one of them with all its strength until it snapped.

'Do you think you should do that?' Miss Turner asked. 'After all, the Commissioner of Police — '

'Is sunk with all hands,' Quirke smiled, turning. 'When I handle a case, Miss Turner, I consider no laws except my own ... I see an external clamp has been fitted here additionally?'

'Formerly there were only the internal clamps,' Harry explained. 'After the police investigation an outer one was fitted.'

Quirke pushed up the clamp and opened the heavy airlock then he stepped into the square, steel-lined 'cell' beyond and switched on the electric light. Its radiance cast on the cold metal walls, floor, and ceiling — upon the cushion, upon the air-conditioning apparatus. There was nothing more.

'Measure up, Molly,' Quirke requested, surveying his huge equator jutting like a sea buttress.

Molly Brayson promptly obeyed, pulling a spring-rule from her pocket. Miss Turner, Harry and Owena drifted to the open doorway to watch.

'Twelve by twelve by twelve,' Molly announced finally.

'A square deal, in fact,' Quirke observed, and simmered with internal laughter, then he roamed to the centre of the cube and looked above him at the electric light. Even with his hand extended over his head he could not reach the brightly gleaming bulb.

'I should hardly think the electric light had anything to do with it,' Harry remarked dryly, at which Quirke turned to him and beamed.

'Never can tell, Mr. de London. There is so little here to work on. A cushion, an air-conditioner, and the electric light. Those are the visible things. Then we have the invisible ones — the possibilities. We have to consider the factor that somehow radiations may have been driven through these dense walls.'

'But they're radiation-proof!' Miss Turner objected. 'How could anything get through?'

'Only in two ways, Miss Turner. Either through an unsuspected fault in the insulation, or else by the use of a wavelength not generally accepted in scientific circles. There are such wave-lengths, as I well know.'

'We can test,' Molly Brayson suggested.

'We can and we shall — later. Meantime I will take the cushion for analysis, since it is the one moveable object. I am rather surprised the Commissioner has left it lying around.'

'It is perfectly innocuous.' Owena said. 'The Commissioner had his experts examine it here on the spot.'

'His experts?' Quirke chuckled within himself and his fat shook ponderously. 'My dear lady, his experts know only routine facts and how to find them. If they came across one which isn't in their training they wouldn't know what to do with it. I am the seeker of the improbabilities. Therein lies my unique talent.'

'Easy, A.Q.,' his secretary warned. 'You're blowing your own trumpet again!'

'Am I? Thank you for reminding me, my dear. Would you be good enough to bring the cushion?'

Quirke returned to the airlock and stepped through it. He puffed gently and looked down on the interested but vaguely doubting faces.

'The overture is complete,' he announced. 'I shall reappear at various times with an assortment of equipment, and I shall also seek an early interview with our friend Rogers. Where can I find him?'

'At the De London residence,' Harry replied, and at that Adam Quirke beamed a farewell and followed the faithful Molly Brayson out of the office.

4

Quirke is baffled

The ambling, dryly quipping man-mountain who presented himself to the outside world, and thereby hid the activity of his analytical mind, was a very different man from the Adam Quirke who worked in his laboratory with the all-understanding secretary-assistant at his side. Here he had no time or need for quips, no need for the leisurely questioning. From his secretary he had nothing to hide.

'It is possible, my dear,' he commented, when he and Molly met in the laboratory after a lunch in town, 'that we may here have a problem after our own hearts. Certainly I never saw one with less to work on. A cushion and air-conditioning apparatus! I ask you!'

'First an analysis of the cushion, I suppose?' the girl asked, and at Quirke's nod she placed the cushion on an insulated stand directly within the focus of a battery of instruments which Quirke began to line up. It was in these instruments that the real genius of the man revealed itself. Every one of them were his own construction, some just modified versions of apparatus in use every day at police headquarters, and others which would have caused many an expert scientist to scratch his head in wonder.

'First, routine dust analysis and see if it tells us anything,' Quirke said, and Molly went to work with the small hand-vacuum sucking the invisible mites and grains from the silk exterior of the cushion and the soft hidden wadding beneath. When she had enough she handed the container to Quirke and he placed it in the spectroscope.

The lights dimmed; the window shutters descended. Light streamed through the slit in the spectroscope and upon the wall screen there appeared the colours of the various elements involved in the burning dust. Quirke read them off from heart and then sighed.

'Ordinary, common or garden dirt,' he commented. 'Back where we were, Molly.'

In a few moments it was daylight again. Adam Quirke stood thinking while the girl cleaned out the spectroscope, pushed the cushion in a huge cellophane bag and labelled it, and then waited for the next.

'Bad start,' Quirke muttered.

'Very. What did you expect to find in the cushion, anyway?'

'Something the experts had missed, naturally. We'd better give it a different workover.'

'X-ray?'

'Uh-huh, though I hardly think there's anything concealed in it.'

In its transparent bag the cushion went through the X-ray process and failed to reveal anything. After which it was put in the focus of ultrasonic and electronic beams, Quirke working on the assumption that if there were any peculiarity in the wadding or the silk of the cushion one or other of the instruments he was using would find it.

He was disappointed. At the end of half

an hour it was clear that the cushion was entirely inoffensive, nor had anything ever been on it. The colourgraph, which would have shown a chemical stain or mark not apparent to the eye or less sensitive instruments, remained undisturbed.

'Which means it is not the cushion,' Quirke said finally. 'File it away, Molly, and let's think of something else.'

'We'd do better, A.Q.,' the girl said, 'if we went along to the cube-room and took our instruments with us — as you said you would. Frankly, I think radiation of some kind put paid to De London. It got through a fault in the insulation.'

'I agree with that possibility, Molly, but how did the killer know there was a fault in the insulation and use it so opportunely? And secondly, why was only De London affected and not the guards? Remember, they were outside the cube-room, and since radiation moves in an outwardly spreading circle — unless specially projected — it would certainly have involved the guards as well. They didn't feel a thing.'

'That,' Molly admitted, bothered, 'is a point.'

Quirke was ridding himself of his smock as he continued speaking. 'I have a hunch on this business, Molly. The killer was damned clever enough to use the insulation in reverse — if we postulate radiation as the cause of death. By that, I mean that if a radiation within the cube-room killed De London — if that radiation was generated in that room and nowhere else — it would not be able to go beyond it because of the insulated walls.'

'True. Then that centres us on the air-conditioning apparatus, the only piece of equipment in the death room.'

'Right!' Quirke gave a nod. 'For that reason we're going to take a close look at the apparatus — at the whole cube-room in fact — and see what the instruments have to say. Whatever is wrong will inevitably reveal itself.'

Quite sanguine that his range of detectors would give him some basis upon which to work, Quirke began to assemble them, and then he and Molly transported them to the big brake which he invariably used when actively engaged on a case. And in the later afternoon he was back again in the private office of the De London building, watched with covert curiosity by Harry and Miss Turner as they endeavoured to conduct their business amidst whirrings, electric flashings, and frequent clangorous hammerings.

It became clear as the time passed that Quirke was most dissatisfied. The detectors, sending ultrasonic beams at the insulated walls of the cube-room, failed to register.

Molly, working inside the room with a magnetic receiver, waited for something to happen as Quirke projected every known radiation at each wall, including cosmic waves. Not one of the radiations passed through, and not one section of wall or roof was overlooked.

'Disturbing, but interesting,' Adam Quirke commented, his moonlike face thoughtful. He was seated like a Buddha on the top of the twelve-foot high cube, the tall stepladders close by.

'No nearer?' Harry asked, glancing up from the desk.

'I am satisfied,' Quirke said, 'that insulation here is one hundred percent efficient. Which precludes any possibility of radiation having been projected from the outside.'

'That leaves only the inside,' Molly said, angling her face upwards from the airlock doorway. 'How about this air-conditioning apparatus? I think there ought to be something there.'

'We'll see. Hold the ladders, m'dear.'

Molly obeyed, and by degrees Quirke lowered his vast bulk down to the floor. Snorting like a grampus and mopping his face he lumbered into the cube-room and looked about him, some unexpected thought chasing through his mind. Evidently it did not resolve for he directed his attention to the air-conditioning machine.

'Standard type,' Molly told him. 'Hutton and Edwards product. I can't see anything unusual about it, and I know the layout well enough. Same as used on all space machines, Absorbs and neutralizes carbonic acid and converts it back to oxy-hydrogen.'

Quirke nodded briefly, eyeing the equipment from every angle. Finally, with a colossal amount of hard breathing, he squeezed his titanic girth into the angle of the corner behind the equipment and in this pinned position contrived to remove the plastic backing. He succeeded eventually and scrutinised the set-up of the equipment's 'entrails'.

'By and large quite normal,' he admitted finally. 'Let me get out and then use the X-ray. We'll have a photo of it and make a microscopic study. If anything unusual presents itself we can come and look at the real thing again.'

'Right!'

Molly left the cube-room and went for the portable X-ray equipment, wheeling it in on its rubber-wheeled stand. In a matter of five minutes the photography had been completed and the plates only awaited development.

'Anything else?' Molly asked, and Quirke eyed her.

'In the midst of such profound complexity, my dear, that is a rather naive question! Anything else indeed! Yes, I want surface scrapings of the walls, ceiling and floor. More spectrum analysis is called for.'

'Right!'

The tireless Molly went to work again. It was not that Adam Quirke believed in making her work hard for her salary, or that he was shirking his own part of the job. The truth was that his mighty size made it impossible for him to indulge in any sustained effort. Quirke was a man of mental accomplishments, not physical.

The noise that followed when Molly switched on the scraper made work impossible for Harry and Miss Turner, as they sat wincing and watching. Quite unconcerned, the din of a dozen buzz saws ringing in her ears, Molly took metallic surface scrapings from the walls and floor, and then grabbed the step-ladders and climbed them so she could deal with the ceiling.

Quirke stood watching. He was not concerned with the vision of Molly's well-moulded legs so blatantly on view; something else was troubling him.

'Damn!' he growled.

'You speak, A.Q.?' Molly looked down at him, hands over her head as she held the scraper with its little repository bag.

'I said 'damn', m'dear. Y'know, I've had a sort of hunch that the ceiling or the electric light might be mixed up in this lot somewhere, but now I see it couldn't be.'

'Why not?'

'Because of the height up. Even I can't reach the lamp at the limit of my height, and I'm far beyond average. You need the stepladders and so would anybody else — I had ideas about a last minute act involving the lighting system, maybe some form of electrocution. It won't fit, though. The killer would have no way of reaching the ceiling unless he dashed back into the office for a chair.'

'Nothing like that happened,' Molly said, scraping vigorously. 'According to the Commissioner the guards testified that nobody monkeyed about with the office furniture. Old man De London was alive and kicking when he shut this airlock — and that was that.'

'Yes — ' Quirke brooded profoundly, his blue eyes squeezed shut. 'That was that. There are hidden scientific implications in this business which I never even suspected.'

After another fifteen minutes Molly had finished her scraping activities and descended from the ladder. She spent a moment or two marking separate bags so the scrapings from any particular portion could be identified, then she glanced at her employer.

'Let us away,' he murmured. 'Doubtless Mr. de London and Miss Turner will be glad to see the back of us.'

Definitely an understatement — they were. And in half an hour Quirke and the girl were back in the laboratory the girl wasting no time in getting the spectroscope into action. In another half-hour the analyses were complete and Quirke was perched on the edge of the bench, sucking at a short and somewhat foul briar pipe.

'We're getting deeper in, Molly,' he muttered.

''Fraid so, boss. Not a single thing that's unusual. Walls, floor and ceiling all show normal tungsten steel spectra — If it's not a silly question, what did you expect?'

'I'd rather hoped this might be a chemical murder, in which case the gases, though apparently dispersed as far as normal detection goes, would have faintly affected the surface electrons of the tungsten steel, enough to slightly alter the normal spectrum reading. But I guessed wrong. Gases did not do it, and we're up a gum tree — Better see what the X-ray plates of the air-conditioner have to tell us.'

Quirke did this photographic task himself and once the prints were finished he and the girl both studied them intently through micro-projectors, to arrive once again at a blank wall. Not in the slightest particular was the cube-room air conditioner any different from those in everyday use on space machines.

'Annoying — and surprising,' Quirke commented, tightening his cushiony lips. 'That wipes out everything except the electric light, and I cannot see where that comes in. Mmmm, maybe I should have told you to bring along the electric bulb and let us have a look at it.'

'I can go back for it.'

'Good! It will give me time to think whilst you're gone.'

It seemed to Molly that when she returned from her quick second visit to the De London edifice that Quirke had not moved in the interval. He was still seated in the broad chair beside the micro-apparatus, his extinguished briar clamped between his teeth,

'I got it,' Molly said, and put it on the bench. 'Normal two hundred watt, though I don't know the manufacturer. New one on me.'

Quirke took the bulb from her and considered it. It was of the clear glass variety, the filament plainly visible within. Embedded in the base of the bulb was the name 'Daylight Electric Company, Swanton. Glos.'

'I hope,' Quirke said, still holding the bulb by its brass bayonet cap, 'that you did not smudge your delectable finger-prints all over the glass?'

Molly smiled. 'You know me better than that, A.Q. I only touched the brass, same as you are doing. How does it signify, though? The Commissioner's boys will surely have fingerprinted everything, including this bulb.'

'Perhaps. I'm none too sure the Commissioner's boys, as you so loosely term them, would think of including the electric lamp. We'd better see for ourselves — The insufflator, please.'

Molly found it and handed it over, together with the necessary powders. Quirke busied himself for a while and then gave a wry smile.

'Clean as a dog's tooth,' he commented. 'If this lamp does play any part in this business the murderer was clever enough to keep his prints away from it, or else cleaned them off afterwards.'

'I know I'm just a moron compared to you, boss, so that is why I cannot see what possible connection the electric light can have with De London's death.'

'I can't see the connection either,' Quirk confessed. 'I am simply left with this as the only possible answer because everything else fails to register. In the realm of the more concrete things this lamp is our last hope. I'm a drowning man clutching at a straw — '

Quirke broke off and bellowed with laughter. Molly Brayson waited patiently, her arms folded, whilst Quirke became purple in the face with merriment and finally coughed and exploded himself into silence again.

'Imagine me clutching at a straw!' he gasped, wiping his eyes.

'We're not sunk yet,' Molly said, irrelevantly. 'How about the very ordinary prospect of poison? Maybe the thing isn't scientific at all but just a straightforward job.'

'Poison!'

'Well, the Commissioner said that old man De London had a medicine dose before he sealed himself up. Rogers gave him the dose. Suppose Rogers is responsible for the killing and the medicine was poisoned? The sort that doesn't show any trace?'

Quirke grinned. 'You're reading too many detective novels, m'girl. Poison without trace! There's no such animal. Besides the pathology report was exhaustive and simply confirmed the M.D.'s certificate — syncope. No reason to suspect foul play.'

Molly became silent; then bethinking herself after she had glanced at her watch she prepared the mid-afternoon cup of tea. Quirke put aside the bulb and thought for a moment or two; then he turned suddenly to the visiphone and dialled the De London edifice number.

Eventually it was Miss Turner's uninteresting face that came into view.

'Oh, Mr. Quirke!' She smiled faintly. 'Can I help you?'

'Possibly yes, possibly no. Can you tell me if you have a lighting contract with the Daylight Electric Company of Swanton, in Gloucester?'

'Er — ' Miss Turner hesitated and reflected for a moment, then she turned away from the screen, saying: 'Just a moment, Mr. Quirke. I'll just make sure.'

Quirke relaxed and hummed a ditty to himself, nodding genially to Molly as she handed him a cup of tea.

'One thing I like about secretaries,' he commented. 'They're so efficient.'

Since Molly did not know whether this was intended to be sarcasm or a compliment she did not respond — then Miss Turner reappeared on the screen.

'Yes, Mr. Quirke, we have a contract with the Daylight Electric Company,' she confirmed. 'Mr. de London arranged it some months ago.'

'The firm,' A.Q. said, 'is not familiar to me.'

'No, it's quite a small one, but for some reason Mr. de London took a fancy to it, chiefly because of the low prices of the lamps, I think. They deal in neon tubes, daylight diffusers and all the rest of it.'

'Mmmm — ' Quirke took a long drink of tea whilst Miss Turner watched him in sour interest through the screen.

'Anything else, Mr. Quirke?'

'Yes. I'd like the name of the managing director of this company.'

Miss Turner looked down at the memorandum she was holding.

'Douglas Jerome,' she said.

'I am indebted to you, Miss Turner, for being so explicit.'

'That's all right — Might I ask where

all this is leading?'

The huge shoulders rose and fell and Quirke beamed genially.

'I haven't the vaguest idea. I'm just slinging around my bait like an inexperienced angler.'

Looking rather irritated, Miss Turner switched off, and with a sigh of satisfaction Quirke slid his ponderous mass into the nearest heavy chair and finished his tea in comfort. Molly, perched somewhat uncomfortably on the edge of the nearby bench, gave him a quizzical look.

'I don't get it, A.Q. Why the interest in the electric light?'

'I told you once, light of my life. I've only the electric light to go on. Just as well to have all particulars of where the lamp came from.'

Silence, and Quirke stared hard into the base of his teacup.

'According to this,' he said, grinning, 'I shall soon meet a thin woman with an angular jaw and positively no sex appeal. Couldn't possibly be you, m'dear, so it must be Miss Turner!'

Molly sighed, took the cup away from him, added it to her own, then went over to the laboratory sink. When she turned again it was to discover her huge employer struggling into his outdoor clothes.

'I feel it incumbent upon me to have words with the police pathologist who examined De London,' he explained, 'to say nothing of an interview with Rogers, who so far has not been added to the jigsaw. You'd better come with me, Molly. You know how helpless I am.'

Molly nodded, grabbed her notebook, and accompanied A.Q. out to his parked car. Before long they were being shown into the private office of the police pathologist, and at length he himself joined them.

'Not often I see you, Quirke,' he smiled, seating himself. 'Still as slender as ever, I see.'

Neither the pathologist nor Molly could speak for a moment, flattened as they were before the hurricane of laughter. Then Quirke wiped his eyes, rumbled once or twice, and came to the point.

'You examined De London. What did you find? Anything unusual?'

'Why, no. You hardly think I would have kept it to myself if I had, do you?'

'I wondered,' Quirke explained, 'if you had perhaps found something inexplicable, and rather than confess to professional ignorance, had kept quiet about it.'

The pathologist smiled rather coldly. 'Knowing you as I do, Quirke, I'll accept that statement. Otherwise I'd be inclined to resent it — And incidentally, why all this sudden interest in De London?'

'It should be obvious, man. I'm trying to find out who had the good sense to send him packing. Damned clever, whoever it was. It's even got me stopped, and that's some admission from Adam Quirke. Look — ' Quirke hunched forward, his huge equator overflowing his knees. 'You're absolutely sure there was nothing unusual about De London's corpse?'

'Nothing unusual at all.'

'What did the bloodstream test show?'

'Only the usual deposits. I did notice,

117

though, that there seemed to be a rather unusual amount of exilene.'

'Exilene? That's a sleeping draught, isn't it?'

'Uh-huh. One of the very latest. Sends you to sleep in about ten seconds, gives you about thirty seconds of extremely deep sleep, and then you wake up fit enough to knock over a spaceship. Good stuff, but mighty potent.'

'And the big noise had traces of it in his system?'

'Definitely, but I imagine that can be accounted for by the medicine he had been ordered to take. There would certainly be exilene in it since he had bad nerves and needed a sedative.'

Quirke sat back again, his equator heaving and his lips tight little bolsters in his full moon of a face. Molly wrote silently, then raised her eyes and waited.

'To need a medicine,' Quirke mused, 'you must have a physical complaint — and the last thing I can imagine De London suffering from was nerves!'

'It was on account of those threats

A.Q.,' Molly reminded him, and she was rewarded with a broad grin.

'A man who practically rules the country getting nerves because of pettifogging threats? No, light of my life, I don't believe it!' Quirke looked at the pathologist. 'You knew De London well enough before his death. Did he ever strike you as a man likely to suffer from nerves?'

'Most certainly he did not!'

'Very well, then. If you don't have 'nerves' in the normal way and yet suddenly develop them there's only one explanation. They have been induced. I think,' Quirke finished, 'a word with the doctor who prescribed De London's medicine is called for.'

'He's Edgar Warren, the neurologist,' the pathologist said. 'Desmond Chambers, mid-City.'

'Much obliged. My delectable secretary and I will pay him a visit within the next hour.'

They did, and found the specialist affable enough even though it was plain he did not quite like the idea of having been caught out without an appointment. Quirke's heavy-handed good nature, however, seemed to take care of everything.

'I'm looking into the cause and effect connected with Mr. de London's death,' Quirke explained. 'I understand he came to you a little while before his decease because his nerves were bad?'

'He did, yes. I overhauled him, and . . . ' Warren hesitated.

'Go ahead,' Quirke invited. 'Professional ethics don't come into this: I want the facts.'

'Well, I found that his nerves and his heart were both suffering from severe overstrain, and I told him so. He admitted he had business worries, even though I suspected there was more to it than that — '

'I see. You prescribed a medicine to be taken three times a day?'

'I did, yes.'

'And there was exilene in it?'

'There was — a fair percentage. I considered it would act as a sedative.'

For some reason Quirke looked vaguely

disappointed; then the mood passed, and he asked another question.

'In your opinion, was De London's sudden nervous state the outcome of natural strain or could it have been induced?'

'Well, I suppose it could have been induced,' the specialist admitted, 'but how would I be able to tell? I merely looked at the effect, not the cause.'

'Quite so,' Quirke surged to his feet, and Molly put her notebook away promptly. 'Thank you so much for your observations, Mr. Warren. I shall look further.'

'No trouble at all, I assure you.' And first the specialist and then the receptionist bowed the pair out. In the car Quirke sat thinking, Molly at the wheel as usual.

'Where to now, A.Q.? To see Rogers?'

'Not just yet. I want to stop in Whitehall and have a word with the Director of Public Control.'

Just why he wanted this Quirke did not explain. Molly guessed it was not so much because he did not intend to — for she was always kept informed of his moves — but because he was following some inner line of thought. What this line was became clear enough to the girl when they were seated in the office of the Director of Public Control, a thin-nosed, acid man responsible for the statistics of births, deaths and marriages, and also having complete authority over the isolation of the unfit and the disposal of the dead.

'Yes, Mr. Quirke, what can I do for you?'

'I require permission to exhume the body of the late Gyron de London.' Quirke spread his fat hands. 'It's as simple as that.'

'Not quite, I'm afraid. There has to be a very good reason for exhumation, Mr. Quirke. Celebrated though you are in the field of scientific investigation, I cannot grant you an exhumation order just on your say-so. Can you supply a convincing reason?'

'Isn't it enough reason that Gyron de London was murdered and that the surest way of proving it is to have his body brought out for further examination?'

The Director frowned. 'You mean you have been engaged to examine the facts of his death?'

'Exactly. Confirmation can be obtained from Mr. De London junior if you care to contact him.'

'No, no. I accept your word, of course. But surely the medical report on Mr. de London's death is sufficient? Is there any reason to doubt the official cause of death?'

'Every reason in the world,' Quirke replied calmly. 'I am of the opinion that De London was murdered in the most ingenious fashion, but I cannot hope to start piecing my case together until I am permitted a full examination of his body . . . I hardly need to add, I think, that any failure on your part to comply with my wishes could be interpreted as an obstruction of justice.'

The Director cleared his throat. 'Er, naturally I shall not place any obstacles in your way, Mr. Quirke.' He reached a form from the desk and scribbled upon it swiftly, finally handing it over. 'There is the necessary permission, but I must inform you that you yourself must remove and return the body. If this were an exhumation granted by Government licence the necessary men would be supplied. As it is I am taking undue advantage of my authority and granting a favour. You understand?'

'Perfectly,' Quirke smiled, rising, 'and many thanks.'

He beamed broadly as he lumbered past the receptionist in the adjoining office; then Molly gave him a doubting look when they were in the car again.

'I hope, A.Q., that you haven't got ideas about my helping with the corpse! I'll do almost anything for you but I put a ban on corpses.'

Quirke chuckled. 'Have no fear, light of my life! Neither of us will go near the body — as far as the exhumation is concerned. I know certain thick-necked and not particularly erudite gentlemen who will be glad to earn a pittance transporting a corpse from the De London mausoleum to my laboratory

— And let us be moving, m'dear. The afternoon has become evening and we have the outstanding factor of Rogers to interview yet.'

Molly nodded and started the car forward down the brightly lighted main street. In fifteen minutes the residence of the De Londons had been gained and a stiff-necked manservant finally sent Rogers into the lounge. As wooden-faced as ever he stood looking as Quirke surveyed him, his cushion of a mouth broken into a genial smile.

'Rogers, the man of all work?'

'Yes, sir. I'm Rogers.'

'My name's Adam Quirke and I'm — '

'Investigating the death of my late master, sir, I suppose?'

Quirke nodded, studying the immovable face.

'Your name is not unknown to me, sir,' Rogers explained. 'Or indeed to anybody who follows the course of scientific crime and its exposure.'

Quirke grinned and looked at his secretary. 'Molly, tell me if I am starting to blush, won't you? Now, Rogers, I have had long conversations with all the others closely connected with your late master, and now I think it's time I had one with you. On the night of his death, what happened? You were the last person to see him alive, I think, except for the guards?'

'Yes, sir. I took him his medicine, as I had been instructed to do, and he seemed in reasonably good spirits.'

'What time was this?'

'Six o'clock, sir.'

'I see. All in all, how long were you with your master?'

'About ten or twelve minutes. When I left him I said I would report at seven in the morning.'

'Mmmm . . . ' Quirke stretched forth his block-like legs and squinted down them. 'Y'know something, Molly? I'm getting no thinner!'

Explosions, an earthquake of laughter, and at last Quirke emerged with streaming eyes and purple cheeks. Then as abruptly as his merriment had commenced it ceased again and his piercing blue eyes pinned the handyman.

'When did you first enter Mr. de London's employ, Rogers?'

'Ten years ago, sir.'

'Did you seek the employment voluntarily?'

'Partly sir, and partly not. It's rather a complicated story, really. At that time I was acting as an assistant to my father, Henry Rogers. He was an experimental scientist, and never made a great deal of money. When he died I was more or less on my beam ends, but since Mr. de London had financed one or two of my father's inventions I thought he might care to take me on. He did, and I became the general handyman.'

'You refer to your father being an experimental scientist. I find that very vague, Rogers. Surely he must have invented something worthwhile in order to have made any living at all?'

'Yes, one or two things.' Rogers' expression was negative. 'Household gadgets, mainly. Never anything big. The ones that might have amounted to something somehow never seemed to hit the jackpot. He died a very dispirited and broken old man.'

'And you, as his son, doubtless had the very human urge to draw the fangs of those responsible for his unsung death?'

Rogers gave a faint smile. 'I must admit that at times such thoughts did occur to me, but what could I do? One very small man with no financial power against the giants of commerce? It was they who smashed my father, sir. They used his brilliance to their own ends. Stole his brain-children, in fact, and he was too preoccupied to notice or do anything about it.'

Quirke reflected; then: 'Was Gyron de London one of these giants of commerce?'

'I have already said he supplied my father with money sir. An enemy would hardly do that . . . '

Quirke struggled to his feet, straightening the deep creases down the front of his clothes; then he gave Rogers a sideways glance.

'Nothing more I can tell you, sir.'

Quirke nodded and gave his disarming smile. 'So far so good, Rogers. If I need you again I'll send for you. Are you ready, light of my life?'

Molly nodded, put away her notebook, and rose to her feet.

5

Element of death

Returning to his home and laboratory Quirke wasted no time in giving his instructions over the visiphone to those 'thick-necked and not particularly erudite gentlemen' who were to carry out the exhumation of Gyron de London, deceased.

'Which means,' Quirke said, when he had a late tea sent into the laboratory for himself and the girl, 'that you can now either quit for the day, m'dear, and go out with your boyfriend or give yourself a beauty treatment — or you can stay with a fat old man whilst he bounces ideas against you until the body comes.'

Molly shrugged. 'I've no ties, so I may as well stay with the fat old man, providing he doesn't ask me to examine that corpse.'

'Seriously, my dear, I won't.' Quirke ate a sandwich with amazing daintiness considering his bulk. 'Now let me bounce a few ideas and see how you react to them. Firstly we have the warnings which purported to come from Mars, and we also have two very likely suspects — even three — who had Martian connections at that time. Namely, young De London and his part-Martian wife and Miss Turner. Right, let us examine them. First Miss Turner could have written, or rather contrived, the warnings and then have had them sent on by a friend at a given time. Correct?'

'Correct,' Molly agreed, pouring out tea.

'Why then,' Quirke asked, reclining in the big chair, 'did she diffuse her activities to include Rogers? Why tell him at the same time?'

'One possibility,' Molly said. 'Maybe — and I'm not trying to be funny, A.Q. — the Turner creature is in love with Rogers and writhed to see how the old man kicked him around. Unable to control her glee at having discovered a watertight way of killing old man De London she had to tell Rogers too, assuring him he would soon be released from slavery.'

'Very ingenious, but the idea of Miss Turner being in love — ' Quirke exploded and nearly choked over his sandwich. In about thirty seconds he came up for air, thumping his barrel of a chest.

'I gather,' Molly said, raising an eyebrow, 'that the idea of Miss Turner being romantic does not convince you?'

'Hardly!' Quirke gulped for breath and mopped his face. 'No, I think you're dead off the beam there my dear. And yet your hypothesis is interesting insofar that it provides the one and only possible reason for Miss Turner being the culprit. Love of Rogers, hatred of her boss's behaviour towards him. On the other hand cutting out the Rogers romantic angle, did she hate her boss so much that she wanted to kill him?'

'Very probably. I imagine she was a girl with bright ideas, then she went into his employ but he smashed the life out of her, same as with everybody else.

Possibly, having reached sour spinster-hood, she spent her off-time figuring out a way of wiping De London off the map.'

Quirke raised a thick finger. 'Ah! Assuming all this m'dear, how do we reconcile the arid index-bound Miss Turner with the brilliant science that undoubtedly put paid to De London?'

'Brilliant science?'

'But definitely! Don't you realize, girl, that even I am stuck in trying to discover the method! That suggests an uncommonly clever scientist. Is Miss Turner that? Hardly!'

'She might be, underneath.'

Quirke shook his bush of white hair. 'She isn't. A clever scientist can't help but unwittingly betray the fact here and there, and that woman hasn't a scientific bone in her body. She's ledger-bound, acrimonious, and unimaginative.'

Molly handed over the filled teacup she had been holding and then gave a little sigh.

'Well, that seems to put paid to Miss Turner as a suspect, unless — Why, yes! Suppose she hired a scientist, or worked in connivance with one? Rogers, for instance?'

'So you're back on the love angle again, are you?'

'Not necessarily. If Miss Turner and Rogers between them — '

'It won't do, Molly! Miss Turner is a woman of the world and unless she did love Rogers — which I regard as definitely unlikely — she would never confide in him far enough to plan the murder of her employer. She'd never feel safe. No, that's out — and so I think is Miss Turner herself as a suspect. Let's move along a little — and another sandwich if you please.'

Molly held forth the sandwiches and Quirke munched contentedly. 'Take Owena de London,' he mumbled. 'I've my own ideas about that Earth-Mars girl, but let's have yours.'

'That's soon done, A.Q. I hate the sight of her.'

'In our business,' A.Q. said, 'we cannot afford to have personal likes and dislikes. Your dislike of her is purely that of one woman to another and has nothing to do with the case itself. Am I right?'

''Fraid so,' Molly admitted. 'I don't like these smart, super-sophisticated women who tell their husbands what to do, and the poor fools do it. You must have noticed how she as good as put words into young Harry de London's mouth?'

'Never mind what she put in his mouth: do you regard her as a likely suspect?'

'Matter of fact I do. From all accounts De London senior hated her for marrying his son and had already shown his displeasure. No reason why Owena shouldn't try and get her own back. On top of that she'd probably have the scientific skill necessary. The Martians are brilliant scientists, as anybody knows. Sort of natural heritage from the original settlers.'

'To the pure Martian, yes — but Owena is not pure Martian. In most respects she's as Earthian as you or I and I don't think we can pin the Martian scientific genius onto her as a matter of course. She struck me as a girl who is really quite delightful, but very disturbed by events and conscious that she must be suspect because of her origin. For that reason her fear sought refuge in that icy sophistication which you found so irksome. Most certainly I cannot picture her as a careful, inhuman killer . . . So, then, to young Harry.'

'Couldn't be less interested,' Molly said. 'At least insofar as being a suspect is concerned. To my mind he's perfectly harmless, impulsive — even hot-tempered — and dominated by Owena. But I'm convinced he did not kill his father. He had good reason, I know, as had Owena, but that doesn't alter my opinion. Besides he doesn't look the type.'

Quirke gave a disapproving glance. 'Doesn't look the type? My dear Molly, when will you learn not to judge from facial appearances. Criminal history shows that many of the most diabolical killers have had faces like a city clerk whilst women in this group have often looked as innocent as the Madonna . . . So you consider that Harry is out? Right. So be it. And what of friend Rogers?'

'Very dubious quantity, A.Q. One of the 'still waters run deep' type. For my money, I wouldn't put anything past him.'

'No . . . ' Quirke considered his sandwich pensively.

'Neither would I. A respectful, inscrutable man, admitting that he has an axe to grind with big business. True, he conveyed the impression that De London had been a friend, not an enemy, but words are cheap. And, as far as I can see he's the only one with any scientific knowledge. I refuse to believe he could work as the Great Henry Rogers' assistant, and be told the many things which a father automatically tells his son, without picking up a great deal of knowledge.'

'Did you say great Henry Rogers, boss?'

'I did. I knew Henry Rogers in the old days, though I did not admit as much to that taciturn young man. Henry Rogers was a genius, but too reticent. I can well understand that big business swindled and crushed him whilst using his ideas. I can even understand his son devoting his life to avenging his father — '

'Which means, A.Q., that you have as good as decided that Rogers is the culprit?'

'In my own mind, yes. Time may prove me wrong, of course, but I don't think it will. The problem here, light of my life, is not so much who committed the murder, but how it was done? And right now I'll be damned if I can nail anything down!'

Quirke sighed to himself, made an end of his sandwiches and tea, then lighted his short briar and sat thinking. Molly busied herself clearing away the cups and plates, knowing from long experience that this was not the time to start talking.

'For the basis of our deductive hypothesis we will accept the fact that Rogers is our man. Right! We accept as his motive the fact that he considered De London contributed in some way to the death of old man Rogers. Right! What, then, did Rogers do to dispose of De London? He somehow produced an effect that has been classified as syncope. What effect? It wasn't radiation, at least, not from outside the cube-room; it wasn't gas because there was no means of installing it, and the air-conditioning plant registers normal — which it would not if gas were in it. The medicine? No, not even that, because the doctor has said he discovered nothing unusual in the corpse. The electric light? The — electric — light . . . '

Quirke fell to musing again, his blue eyes narrowed.

'I keep coming back to that,' he muttered. 'I am enough intrigued by it to learn all about the firm who manufactures the bulbs for the De London edifice, of which the cube-room electric bulb was one. Tomorrow I must go and see them. The only way we can sink our teeth into anything on this job, Molly, is for me to examine the corpse by myself and see if I can find anything unusual.'

'Just what do you hope to find?'

'I want to find something to account for the ten minutes when Rogers was with his master. I remain convinced that something happened in that ten minutes which will be the answer to the whole thing.'

Molly reflected, frowning. Quirke gave

her a glance and then stabbed the stem of his briar towards her.

'Look at it this way, Molly. Whatever killed De London had somehow to be placed in the cube-room, and it certainly would not be put there in advance in case it was discovered — and besides, there was no place where anything could be concealed. We are faced with two alternatives: either something was given to De London in his medicine, which later produced death from apparent syncope — although that doesn't seem likely to judge from the doctor's report — or else the electric light came into it.'

'But how, boss?' Molly demanded, bewildered, gazing at the bulb lying on the bench. 'What on earth could the electric light do?'

'I've no idea. I am only centring on it because it was the only other 'gadget' — if I may call it such — in that very bare room. If, though, something was done to the electric light how in the name of Satan did Rogers manage it with the ceiling twelve feet high and De London right beside him?'

Molly relaxed, plainly beaten. Quirke bit hard on his pipe, then picked the bulb up again and studied it.

'So far,' he said, 'I've only examined this thing for fingerprints. I might do worse than examine it completely — the interior I mean — whilst I'm waiting for De London's corpse to be brought.'

His mind made up he went to work, first unsealing the normal glass outer casing. When he had done this he peered intently at a minute ashy deposit in the base of the pear-shaped glass.

'Queer,' he muttered. 'I wonder how that got there?'

He shook some of the dust onto a slide from the spectrograph and then switched off the lights. The spectrum reading of the ash immediately appeared on the wall-screen.

'Copper and tungsten,' Quirke said, reading off the colours. 'Wonder if there's anything in the invisible spectrum?'

He switched in the automatic coupler by which radiations outside the visual range — beyond the infra-red or violet ends — could reveal themselves. And the surprising thing was that in the lower infra-red end there was a decided reaction!

'Ah, success!' Quirke murmured. 'That means that, when this ash was in solid form, before being burned out, it was made up of metallic elements containing copper and tungsten — and maybe a gaseous element which — ' Quirke thought and shook his head. 'No, not a gaseous element otherwise it could not have deposited itself as ash. A metallic element, fused in with the copper and tungsten. A rare metallic element indeed with no ordinary spectrum, but one which only has a reading well below infra-red.'

'Which means heat,' Molly said, pondering.

'Uh-huh, to a great extent. Light of my life, I do believe we are getting somewhere! A metal that has a spectrum reading below the red is fascinating and unique. Let me see now . . . ' Breathing like a walrus Quirke hauled himself forward and looked at the temperature reading. It showed the invisible spectrum to be in the region of 200 degrees F.

'More interesting than ever!' he commented. 'To my mind there is no metal which answers this description, so whoever discovered it has a monopoly, at present. The thing to do is discover what the metal is and where it came from — and above all what it does. That can wait a moment, though. Let us see if this filament is all it is supposed to be.'

In a second or two he had removed it from its electrode rest and put it through the usual spectrographic tests. It emerged from them classified as perfectly normal tungsten steel filament with the usual protective long-burning coating.

'Any nearer?' Molly asked, her eyes bright.

'Somewhat, my love.' Quirke brooded, chewing his pipe stem. 'But for the chance of analysing this microscopic dust we'd have been as far away as ever. I venture to think that the killer — or shall I say Rogers? — trusted to luck that the dust would never be noticed. To the careless worker it might not have been since a slight dust flaking of tungsten often falls from a lamp filament. But my guess is that originally this lamp had two filaments! The one normal, existing as an inner core filament, and the other made of a composite of copper, tungsten, and the unknown element . . . '

Molly was silent, waiting for the next. Quirke drew hard at his extinguished pipe.

'Not much I can do if I start searching for a rare metal,' he said finally. 'Might take me the rest of my life. The better way will be to interview the managing director of the light company and see if I can glean anything worthwhile. But we're on to something, Molly, I'm convinced of it.'

'Seems like it.' Molly made a restless movement. 'Will there be anything else, boss, or have you finished bouncing your ideas against me?'

'For the moment I've finished bouncing — ' Quirke broke off and surged and exploded with merriment. Molly put on her hat and coat, by which time the earthquake had ceased.

'That I should ever finish bouncing!' Quirke gulped, tears running down his cheeks. 'Dammit, I never do anything else! Quite — quite the funniest thing I've said for some time.'

'Yes, A.Q.,' Molly agreed dutifully. 'Shall I be here at the usual time tomorrow?'

'I hope so. By then I'll have discovered something about the De London cadaver.'

Molly took her departure and for the next half-hour Quirke sat thinking and smoking, to be finally interrupted as the exhumed body of De London was carried into the laboratory, still inside its coffin. The thick-necked, burly men carrying the coffin laid it on the broad trestle table, which Quirke had cleared specially for the purpose.

'There it is, Mr. Quirke.' The tallest of the men motioned briefly. 'Anything else?'

'Not at the moment, Nick. I'll want you to take the body back later, but I'll give you a ring.'

'Okay, Mr. Quirke. Good night.'

'Night,' Quirke murmured absently, picking up a screwdriver and going to work on the coffin lid.

* * *

When Molly arrived at the laboratory around 9.30 the following morning she found Quirke looking as though he had never moved from the position in which she had left him the previous evening. He was half-lounging beside the bench, his hair tousled even more than usual, and his pipe clenched between his teeth. The air was warm and smelled vaguely of powerful antiseptics.

Molly took off her coat and glanced about her. There was no sign of the De London cadaver. She took off her hat and moved to where her employer stood.

'Remember me, A.Q.?' she enquired, and he stirred and beamed upon her.

'Remember you! Light of my life, I can never forget you. But let me apologise for my frowsy appearance. I've had very little sleep, no shave, a very meagre breakfast, and am somewhat weary from excess of thinking. But I have taken a big stride forward in the De London mystery.'

'You got the cadaver all right, then?'

'I did, and spent most of the night

making examinations and tests. I can well see why the verdict was heart failure: a doctor of the normal school could hardly come to any other conclusion. But it was the bloodstream that I found most interesting. It contained not only traces of exilene, but also of miopadrax. And the miopadrax was greatly in excess of the exilene and noticeable not only in the bloodstream but also in the lungs, stomach and intestines.'

Molly looked somewhat blank. 'What in the world's miopadrax? I've never heard of it.'

'No blame attaches for that. Few people have, unless they be well versed in chemistry, as I hope I am. Miopadrax is a drug with a vague relationship to one-time adrenalin. It produces extreme stimulation and well-being — for a time. Afterwards, when reaction sets in, intense depression occurs, verging on melancholia. If it doesn't get that far it produces morbid and quite baseless fears.'

'In other words, nerves?'

'Right!' Quirke beamed with satisfaction. 'My favourite girlfriend is extra bright this morning. Nerves! That's it exactly. Now you know what I was fishing for when I asked that pathologist if De London's condition could have been induced. It's perfectly obvious now that he was made ill deliberately . . . '

'By the medicine, you mean?'

Quirke shook his mane of white hair sadly. 'Molly, you are not so bright as I thought. How could the medicine produce the condition when it existed before the medicine?'

'Sorry!' Molly looked contrite. 'I hadn't thought of that. How, then, was this miopasomething administered?'

'There's one perfectly obvious solution — by means of cigars. To make sure of this possibility I impregnated a cigar with miopadrax solution during the night — not in a very great quantity — and then I smoked it. My test showed me I had all the symptoms of nerves and depression. They passed off after a while, but had I smoked cigars constantly, as De London did, and had each one been heavily impregnated, I'd very soon have become a nervous wreck.'

Molly perched herself on the bench edge. 'So that's it! Doctored cigars to produce nerves and make a medicine necessary — But what for? What has that got to do with murdering De London?'

'That,' Quirke said, 'was what I asked myself, and the more I thought about it the more I appreciated the diabolical cunning of the mind behind the whole thing. The reason for the induced nerves was, I believe, to make an excuse to see De London at the last moment before he locked himself in the cube-room. An excuse to fix the gadget — whatever it was — that killed him.'

'You mean that the killer — or Rogers, if you prefer — caused De London to have nerves, knowing that he would seek medical advice?'

'That is my belief, and Rogers would also guess that a medicine would be prescribed, possibly containing the very potent exilene. Most medicines are prescribed for three times a day, and I think Rogers relied on that possibility knowing also that the task of reminding De London about the medicine times would probably fall to him. That, I repeat, gave him the normal excuse to see his master a short while before he locked himself in his cube-room.'

'Very ingenious,' Molly admitted, nodding in faint admiration. 'He provided both cause and cure to serve his own ends?'

'So I think. I am satisfied from my examination of the corpse that neither exilene nor miopadrax caused death, therefore the murder was not committed by way of the medicine. That brings us back to the lamp, and before I can go much further in that direction I must see the Daylight Electric Company in Swanton, and that is where I intend to head this morning. Naturally you will alleviate the monotony of the journey, my love, by being present to pilot the helicopter.'

'I'll get it out of the roof-garage,' Molly said, heading for the door, and Quirke observed that he would join her the moment he had had a shave.

The 'moment' proved to be fifteen minutes later when he squeezed his colossal bulk into the helicopter's cabin and Molly started up the powerful atomic motor. To Swanton, in Gloucestershire, from London was only a brief hop and in another twenty minutes the managing director of the Daylight Electric Company — a small but obviously efficiently run concern in the heart of the countryside — was welcoming his two visitors

'I'm Adam Quirke,' Quirke explained, struggling down into an armchair and puffing bronchially. 'My secretary and right hand — Miss Brayson. My reason for visiting you is mainly a police matter.'

'Really?' The managing director, a sharp-nosed man with exceptionally well-brushed hair, looked vaguely uncomfortable. 'I'm afraid I cannot just accept your word for that, Mr. Quirke. Shouldn't you have a warrant-card, or something?'

'If I were an ordinary policeman, yes — but I'm not.' Quirke spread his hands. 'I am a scientific specialist in crime, commissioned by the De Londons to investigate the true circumstances connected with the death of Gyron de London.'

'Indeed? Very interesting, of course, but what has that to do with me, or my firm?'

'Your firm? You are the owner of it?'

'That is the usual capacity of a managing director, is it not?'

'There are exceptions,' Quirke said amiably. 'In certain cases the owner of a business does not appear himself but leaves everything to a managing director. I fancied that might be so in this case.'

'No, Mr. Quirke. I am the sole owner of this business, and anything you may have to say concerning it should be directly addressed to me.'

'Mmmm, I see.' Quirke reflected, then: 'I understand that you supply the De London enterprise with lamps, neon tubes, and all the usual lighting apparatus?'

'We do, yes. A very good contract it is, too.'

Silence. The managing director was looking puzzled. He pushed across the cigarettes but Quirke shook his white mane of hair and lighted his briar instead.

'Did you ever hear of a man called

Rogers?' he asked. 'And, mind you, sir, this is strictly confidential.'

'Rogers? Rogers? Not that I can recall, but then, we have a pretty large staff. I can probably check on it for you. You mean on the working staff?'

'I mean anywhere in this organisation.'

The managing director switched on the intercom and gave instructions for the names of the firm's employees, past and present, to be checked. After a while the answer came through.

'No sign of anybody with that name, sir. I've gone through the list from the day the firm began business.'

'Right, Mason. Thanks.'

Quirke sat scowling to himself, and Molly guessed that for the moment he was up a gum tree. Then his slowly dawning smile showed that a new line of approach had occurred to him. He turned his sharp blue eyes on the managing director once again.

'Does your product appear in the shops in the usual manner or are you exclusively contractual? By that I mean, do you supply your lighting equipment on contract only, or is there general sale?'

'General sale. Any electrical shop has our product, and so do the big stores.'

'Ah!' Quirke fought his way to his feet and snorted for breath. 'That, sir, solves my little problem, I think. You have been most co-operative — and I feel that I should warn you that at a later date your firm is liable to come in for a great deal of publicity, and not entirely favourable publicity either.'

'Oh? There's nothing wrong with our material; I'll swear to that!'

'I've no doubt of that, but one particularly clever scientist has used one of your lamps, with your firm's name on it, to mature a most villainous scheme. For that reason, when the story is told, your lamps are bound to be mentioned.'

'I'll take action if there is any reflection upon us!'

'It will hardly be necessary when the time arises,' Quirke smiled. 'The person whom you would have to indict will then be impaled by the full panoply of justice. However, my thanks, sir, and good day. Coming, Molly?'

'Ready, A.Q.'

★　★　★

'What was all that about, anyway? Just kind words, or did something really occur to you?'

'Something really occurred to me. My first belief was that perhaps Rogers was the secret owner of the Daylight Electric Company, by which means he would be able to get at the lamps in the factory any time he chose and, perhaps, fashion one to his own design. That belief went down the drain, to be replaced with the only possible answer — that Rogers bought a perfectly normal lamp in a store somewhere and then secretly altered it to suit his own purposes.'

'Without a laboratory or equipment? That's stretching things a bit, A.Q., isn't it?'

'I don't believe Rogers is without a laboratory,' Quirke replied. 'What about his father's laboratory? I know he had one, beautifully equipped, and I also know where it was located. It's more than possible that Rogers never sold out to a scientist but used it — and still uses it, maybe — himself.'

'That,' Molly admitted, 'really is something. What do we do, then? Take a look at this laboratory and see if it's still in the name of Rogers?'

'That seems to be the best course, yes, but we'd better do it at night, and also at a time when we can be sure that Rogers is not likely to walk in on us.'

'No guarantee of that. In his off-duty time he might turn up at any hour.'

'Not if we make sure that he doesn't,' Quirke grinned. 'I'll tell you what we'll do, Molly. You took down in full the statements made by Harry and Owena de London. Didn't you?'

'Every word.'

'Good! When we get back home have those statements made out in duplicate. Then 'phone Harry and Owena to come over to my place this evening and sign the statement after reading them through. That's normal police procedure, anyway, and they won't suspect a thing. Rogers will be compelled to bring them in the helicopter, wait for them, and take them home again. In that time I'll be busy at the laboratory, assured that he can't walk in on me.'

'Think of everything, don't you?' Molly sighed, and Quirke chuckled until an upsurge of phlegm stopped him . . . and in a few more minutes they had reached home, and the laboratory, and Molly immediately went to work as instructed. Meantime Quirke visiphoned Harry de London and secured his rather grudging assent to come that evening, with his wife, to sign the necessary statements.

'Just routine, you understand,' Quirke explained genially, studying Harry's troubled face in the screen. 'It does not imply any direct suspicion to you or your wife.'

'How about Miss Turner and Rogers? Do they have to sign statements too?'

Quirke reflected swiftly. Here was an ideal chance to pin down Rogers completely.

'Rogers, yes,' he agreed. 'He may as well since he'll be piloting you over here.

We'll get around to Miss Turner later.'

'All right, Mr. Quirke. We'll be there.'

Quirke nodded and switched off. Molly glanced around from her machine upon which the statements were being automatically printed and transcribed from her original notes.

'Rogers' statement as well?' she asked.

'If you please . . . ' Quirke lumbered over to the bench and picked up the lamp, which he was convinced had been the cause of the tycoon's death. Thoughtfully he went through an examination — an examination purely of the eye since he had already made a microscopic and spectrographic analysis.

'Tell you one thing, light of my life . . . ' Quirke made the observation after a long interval. 'This brass cap on this lamp is of considerable age. I never noticed it before in my interest in the lamp proper. And what is left of the glass pear now I've finished shattering it — the part left welded into the brass, I mean — is comparatively new. An old cap, yet new glass. Mmmm — very interesting.'

'Can't be that old, A.Q.' Molly turned from her task to look at him. 'The Daylight Company wouldn't put excessively old brass caps on their lamps. They'd go out of business.'

Quirke did not reply. Apparently discovering something of further interest in the lamp's bayonet cap he put it in the vice-jaws and then studied it intently through a powerful lens. Wheezing and puffing he presently straightened up and jerked his head.

'Come here a moment, light of my life, and take a look at this . . .'

Inwardly wishing she did not have to keep being interrupted Molly obeyed, putting her eye to the microscope and studying the top end of the brass cap with its two lead electrode points and black plastic filling.

'Well?' Quirke asked, rubbing his chubby hands in anticipation. 'See anything?'

'Nothing unusual, boss. Should I?'

'Should you! You can do better than that, Molly. Can't you see a badly filled and extremely small hole in the plastic?'

Molly looked again and at last managed to discover what Quirke meant. In one place, slightly to the right of where the main stem of the lamp's filament support was imbedded, there was a rough circular speck of material darker than the surrounding plastic insulation filling. But as far as Molly was concerned it did not mean a thing.

'Yes, I see it,' she confirmed, straightening up and rubbing her eye. 'What does it mean, anyway?'

'It means, m'dear, that a hole has been driven through there and afterwards refilled. Now, let us view the business step by step. First — new glass with the Daylight Company name on it, a perfectly genuine pear-glass. But fitted into an old brass cap. Would a firm turn out a lamp like that? No! What is the answer?'

'I'd say that somebody used an old brass cap and, from a new lamp, took the Daylight pear-glass and carefully welded it to the old brass cap.'

'Good girl! And the hole in the insulation?'

'I dunno.' Molly frowned. 'That beats me.'

'Surely it is plain enough?' Quirke asked. 'In fitting a new glass round the filament the original gas would disperse. Fresh gas would have to be put in. So, a hole is drilled through the insulation, argon gas is pumped in to the required density, the hole is resealed — and there it is. But the resealing has been done with material slightly darker than the insulation, which is a direct giveaway.'

'It's all very complicated,' Molly said, bewildered.

'Not when you follow it step by step. Rogers has a master lamp which — by a process we don't yet know — does something. He has had it some time, hence the age of the brass cap. He wants to make the lamp look normal and up to date, and particularly wants it to match the lamps usually used by the De Londons. So what does he do? Buys a normal Daylight lamp, removes the glass pear, welds it onto the brass filament fixture he already has, pumps in argon gas — and there it is. Very clever: I must hand that much to him.'

Molly sighed as she returned to her keyboard. 'How he must have hated De London to go to so much trouble!'

'Perhaps it was not hatred which drove him on so much as his love of scientific achievement: He wanted to produce a foolproof murder and very nearly managed it. Indeed,' Quirke finished, frowning, 'he'll get clean away with it unless I can discover what that missing element is which is spectrographically beyond the red end . . . '

For the moment, however, there was nothing more he could do. His next moves could only come after he had had a chance to inspect the Rogers laboratory, granting it still existed — and that would not be until evening. So, as was characteristic of him, Quirke did not wear his highly trained mind to bits for the rest of the day. Instead he interested himself in some complicated chemical experiment, whilst Molly marvelled silently at his mental detachment. Then, towards eight o'clock, the time for the De Londons and Rogers to arrive, Quirke took his departure, leaving word with Molly to apologise for his absence and explain that urgent business had called him away. She took her instructions with complete assurance, quite confident that she could handle the visitors, and delay them in every possible way.

For his journey to the Rogers laboratory, which as he recalled it lay at the north of the city, Quirke used his spacious car instead of the helicopter. This way there was no chance of him passing the De Londons en route ... And to his immense satisfaction the laboratory was still there and looking no different from the time when he had formerly visited it during the lifetime of Henry Rogers.

But there remained the question: was the laboratory still a Rogers' possession or had it changed hands in the interval? Quirke was not the kind of man to allow this imponderance to stand in his way so, with his usual immense geniality — which always succeeded in hiding his real purpose — he managed to wheedle from the owners of the properties near the Rogers' laboratory all the information he needed. Yes, the laboratory was still owned by a Mr. Rogers. Old man Rogers himself had been dead for some time but his son had taken it over. No, he was not often seen at the laboratory — just now and again.

Which was all Quirke needed to know. He allowed an hour to pass after making his enquiries so that any suspicions that might have been aroused could have time to subside — then by way of the back route he gained the yard at the rear of the laboratory and advanced silently. He was thankful for the moonlessness of the night for his bulk was such that any intent watching eyes might descry him.

Keeping close to the high wall he headed for a lower window, opening it with an electronic cutter, which silently melted away a portion of the glass and allowed him to reach inside and pull back the catch. After which he spent a somewhat anxious five minutes struggling into the gloom of the room beyond. Here he paused only long enough to fuse new glass invisibly into place — by electrically stretching the orbital electrons of the rest of the pane and causing it to become 'elastic' and correspondingly thinner in texture — then he closed the shutters and switched on the light.

The investigation he made was thorough and minute and because of the scientific instruments he carried with him nothing stood in his way. Locked steel cabinets and an up-to-date safe were undetectably opened and their contents examined and photographed on microfilm. Then the benches and tools were carefully scrutinised. Altogether Quirke took nearly two hours over his task, keeping one ear constantly cocked for signs of interruption . . . But none came. And at last, satisfied that he had found out everything that was possible, Quirke departed silently by the normal door, magnetically shooting the steel catch into position from the outside. There was nothing to show that he had ever been.

It was nearly eleven when he landed back in his own laboratory to find Molly Brayson lounging in one of the big chairs and idling through a cigarette. She looked up expectantly as the Colossus came in.

'Any luck, boss?'

'In one way, yes; in another, no.' Quirke was looking faintly disappointed as he tugged off his overcoat. 'Fix up some supper for the pair of us and I'll tell you all about it.'

Molly obeyed promptly, taking ready prepared sandwiches from the electronic cooler and quickly reheating the coffee in the radiant energy coil. Then she seated herself and Quirke heaved and grunted down into a chair opposite her.

'On the one hand,' he said, 'I came across a very sketchy, but nevertheless understandable, formula, relating to invisible heat radiations — which carries us beyond the red end of the spectrum — but on the other hand I didn't find a single thing to suggest that Rogers might have been at work on a lamp.'

'Explainable by the fact that he doubtless cleared everything away after him.'

'But why should he? He has no reason to think that anybody might explore his laboratory. Perhaps he might have made a general clean-up after his activities, but even that would not account for there not being the least trace of glass shards or brass filings, or plastic droppings. Indeed, most of the instruments — which he would have had to use for his glass-modification stunt — appear not to have been used for ages. The laboratory is nearly a museum piece . . . '

'Then he perhaps did the job somewhere else — maybe in the De London garage or one of the estate workshops.'

'He'd never do that, Molly — not with a laboratory of his own in which to work unhindered.' Quirke sat for a moment with his brows knitted whilst he chewed a sandwich; then he continued: 'On the other hand I did find a formula relating to invisible heat radiations, together with a number of rough sketches which, believe it or not, look very much to be like the embryonic designs of a lamp — '

'They do?' Molly's face brightened considerably.

'I micro-photographed the formula and drawings, but I can give you the outline. The formula refers mainly to a metallic element that exists in the sun in enormous quantities, but as a gaseous element, of course. On Earth it does not exist in the pure state — and therefore isn't classified — but it can be extracted in small quantities from uranium, magnesium, and one or two other well known elements, all of which also exist in the sun in gaseous form.'

'Naturally everything that exists in gas form in the sun must exist on Earth, too,' Molly said. 'Earth is a child of the sun and contains the same elements, but in solid form.'

'True enough,' Quirke nodded. 'It appears from this long and complicated formula that this unusual metal always combines with some other element in the process of cooling, hence the reason for it being found in uranium and so forth. I gather the quantities are so minute that no scientist — except Rogers — has considered them worth troubling about as a commercial proposition. Rogers, though, discovered the extraordinary electrical and radioactive properties of this element, which he called K-74, purely to apply a scientific label.'

'Very technical and very complicated,' Molly said, 'but where does it all lead? Has it anything to do with the mystery lamp?'

'I think it may have.' Quirke nodded slowly. 'What I intend to do is extract this element from the uranium, magnesium, and other elements which I have in the laboratory here — and extract it in the manner described by Rogers in his notes. Then I'll see what happens when the element is made to carry an electric current . . . '

'You keep speaking of Rogers' formula,' Molly remarked, musing. 'Are you referring to the old Rogers or the young one?'

'I'm talking about the great Henry. Only a man like Henry Rogers, one of the greatest and most acknowledged scientists of all time, could have thought of a formula like that. Besides, the formula, sketches, and all the rest of it, are done in ox-gall ink and the tintometer I carried with me showed the ink to be some ten to fifteen years old. No doubt that Henry Rogers discovered K-74.'

'And his son cashed in on it by devising

some sort of electric lamp with K-74 mixed up in it?'

'That's a reasonable assumption at the moment, light of my life . . . And you're looking sleepy. Best thing you can do is go home and preserve your beauty. Since I don't need to preserve mine I'll probably work all night.'

Quirke bellowed and roared through a paroxysm of merriment, gurgling something about 'beauty sleep' at intervals. By the time he had come up again for air Molly was in her outdoor things and looking at him impassively.

'See you tomorrow, boss,' she said, and with a nod he got to his feet.

'Yes, m'dear. And — by the by, how did things go with our friends tonight? The statements signed?'

'Perfectly. All three of them were very taciturn — In fact, Owena was openly insulting, but as you once pointed out that was perhaps only put up as a sort of defensive screen. Rogers looked ill at ease, but whether it was because he was with his employers and accordingly felt awkward, or whether he sensed he might be signing something to indict him, I don't know. Anyway, I kept them occupied as long as I could.'

'You did admirably . . . Sleep well.'

Molly went on her way and Quirke lighted his briar in preparation for an all-night session. And an all-night session it was. Part of the time Quirke was in heavily insulated armour as he experimented with radioactive materials and, by cyclotron process, extracted the almost infinitesimal K-74 from the uranium and other elements he had stored in the laboratory.

It was towards four in the morning before he achieved the effect he wanted, and the outcome of a battering of electrical forces finally produced a small greyish lump of what seemed to be metal. It looked like pig iron, except that it had a much more crystalline quality. Here for the time being Quirke stopped his activities and instead retired to his largest chair to ponder the formula, sketches, and notes which by this time had been photographically restored to their original size.

Daylight came, and Quirke was still pondering. He took time out to shave, dress and have breakfast — which included a dose of powerful restorative — then he returned to the laboratory to renew his attack, and found that Molly had arrived once more for the day's work.

'Place is mighty stuffy, A.Q.,' she remarked, snapping back the shutters and opening the ventilators. 'In fact it smells of an all-night session. Am I right?'

'Quite right.' Quirke spoke in a faraway voice and Molly looked at him enquiringly.

'How far did you get, boss?'

'Far enough to extract K-74, which is a good deal. This morning I intend to experiment with it. I waited until you came because I felt that you would like to be in on it. As to the stuff itself . . . ' Quirke relapsed into thought.

'Yes?'

'When it is heated to maximum it produces a radiation, but what that radiation does I don't yet know. I have also discovered something else, from the Rogers' notes which I photographed.'

Molly waited, interested.

'Rogers actually invented a lamp, based on K-74. He invented it many years ago and made a full-scale model. It was intended for defence purposes and, possibly, is now pigeonholed somewhere in the War Office. The lamp was based on the simple scientific principle that the invisible radiation of a normal electric lamp is eight times in excess of the visible. That is to say that eight times as much radiation is actually emanated than is ever turned to account. That includes heat and other types of radiation. K-74 on the other hand has visible radiation in the form of light when current is passed through it — or I assume so from the notes, since I haven't actually tried it yet — but the invisible radiations from it are in the neighbourhood of thirty-six times plus!'

Molly looked surprised. 'You mean that thirty-six times as much radiation as is visible is generated?'

'Yes — and what kind of radiation it is I don't yet know, but I suspect it may be lethal. For two reasons — one, that the

173

lamp in its first stages was used for defence offering; and two, that a similarly constructed lamp, or even the same lamp perhaps, caused the death of Gyron de London. We're dealing in deep things, m'dear, in the creation of a scientific genius whose wonderful idea has, in later years, been turned to cunning crime.'

'And you believe that Rogers the younger built such a lamp from his father's original sketches and plans, or perhaps used the original lamp and converted it to make it look modern?'

'I'd like to think so.' Quirke's brows knitted. 'I said earlier that our problem is not so much who killed De London as how. Now I rather wish I had not been quite so casual. I accepted Rogers as the murderer because logic and circumstances seemed to combine to indicate him. Now I begin to wonder. The absence of signs of activity in the laboratory for one thing, and for another, if the original lamp was used — as seems very likely judging from the age of the brass cap — how the devil did Rogers ever get it from the War Ministry?'

'Are you sure it went to the War Ministry, boss?' Molly smiled a little. 'Sometimes, boss, a secretary earns her money, and I mostly earn mine by reminding you of everyday facts which your far-reaching scientific prowess overlooks. Suppose — and this is only a theory, mind you — that Rogers took his invention to a financier to begin with? He'd get better terms than from the War Ministry, or at least he probably would.'

'Meaning, light of my life, that the said financier might have been tycoon De London?'

'As well as anybody.'

Quirke breathed bronchially and nodded his mane of white hair. 'Excellent logic, m'dear. It would explain how Rogers could perhaps get the lamp. He certainly never would if the War Ministry had it . . . Well, to work! Let us see what K-74 can do. Get out two white mice, will you, and fix them on the experimental tray.'

Molly did as bidden. Meanwhile, working from a distance with heavily insulated tongs, and himself wearing a protective covering, Quirke went to work on the lump of mystery metal, a solidified gas whose prototype lay in the flaming incandescence of the sun, and finally sealed it in a matrix. The matrix was not insulated in any way so that the radiations from the lump could pass out freely once it was electrified. The rest of the task was simply a matter of wiring the matrix to the normal power feed.

'Right!' Quirke exclaimed. 'Into your protective suit, Molly, and we'll see what happens. Our white mice will tell us all we want to know, and for some reason I always feel a perfect fiend at having to put those harmless little devils through the hoops.'

'Well, we can't go through the hoops every time,' Molly said, stepping into her suit.

'I couldn't go through one at any time!' Quirke choked, and a full minute's interval had to be declared whilst he surged and rolled out of his paroxysm of laughter. Then, seeing that the girl was ready, he dropped his visor in place over his grinning, empurpled face.

Crossing over to the switchboard he snapped on the current, and immediately he became the intent scientist instead of the man mountain reduced to hysteria by a vaguely humorous comment. In silence Molly stood beside him, a shapeless figure in her insulated covering. Together they watched the lump of K-74 begin to heat, like the element of a radiator coming slowly to maximum.

Quirke turned aside and looked at the instruments, which were registering the lamp's emanations. They showed a considerable heat was being generated, and also one particular vibration which, being outside the normal known radiations, was playing havoc with the delicate instrument trying to cope with it.

This was no longer a matter for instruments. The white mice were showing exactly what was happening. They were scurrying wildly on the experimental tray directly beneath the K-74. Quirke watched them, then Molly gripped his arm as the mystery lump gradually began to give forth light. And what light! It was at first the normal glow of an electric lamp, but as time passed it became brighter and brighter, tinging to blue, until the whole laboratory was soaked in a pallid, unwavering glare that destroyed every shadow. There was considerable heat also, but not enough to make the place catch fire.

'Good job these vizors are insulated,' Quirke muttered. 'That kind of light, to say nothing of the unknown radiations also being given off, would probably have destroyed our sight by this time otherwise.'

Molly nodded, watching in fascination. Until at length the glare became too intolerable and she had to turn away. Quirke too found it too much for him, but his determination to see the experiment through restrained him from switching off the current. So the light continued building up into an intolerable effulgence — then sudden extinction, like some ultra-powerful firework burned out. There remained a glowing red-hot lump of metal that very suddenly broke into fragments and then fell as fine dust onto the motionless mice below.

Quirke struggled out of his suit and then mopped his face. Molly, her hair damp and straggling down her forehead, gave him a questioning glance. He saw what she meant. The mice were quite plainly dead, but it had not been heat or light that had killed them. The generation of heat had not been anywhere near proportionate to the amount of light — and light alone does not kill unless built up into an unbearable photonic pressure.

The fact remained: the mice were dead. Quirke went over to them, but he did not immediately touch them. First he used a detector to discover whether or not they were electrified or radioactive, but neither appeared to be the case.

'In these two dead rodents I think we have a repetition of the something which killed De London,' Quirke said at last. 'The next obvious move is to dissect one of them and discover what caused death.'

So he went to work whilst Molly cleared away the apparatus. After about half-an-hour Quirke disposed of the mouse which he had dissected and sat in thought.

'Anything?' Molly questioned.

'I think so. Fix some coffee, sweetheart, and then I'll tell you — if I can.'

Molly did so — only a few minutes' work, then Quirke looked at her.

'The mouse I examined died from what seems to be syncope,' he said. 'Presumably the other mouse died from the same cause. And so did De London — but what caused the syncope? That is my point. In this case — more clearly apparent in the delicate organism of the mouse than in the cadaver of De London — the indications are that intense shock from the brain produced it. Only one thing could produce that shock — the radiations from the electrically charged K-74. Or, more specifically, one radiation in particular. A radiation that is approximately five percent light and ninety-five percent vibration. It is a form of calorescence, by which only the merest fraction of the radiation is in the visible spectrum. The rest is in the invisible, below the red end. And like many radiations which exist down there, it affects human tissue adversely.'

Quirke sipped his coffee slowly, no longer noticing that Molly was even there. His thoughts were plainly probing into the scientific deeps and he spoke as they crystallized.

'The sun,' he resumed, 'gives forth endless radiations, the only one we notice being of the order of light. There is also heat of course, but that we feel and do not see. There are also X-rays, gamma, alpha and beta radiations. The whole works, together with one subtle radiation low down in the red end, and of tremendous wavelength, which is responsible for the many cases of heat prostration, sunstroke, and syncope on a hot summer day. Offhand, one says somebody died because of the heat. It is never that. Heat of itself, as far as the sun is concerned anyway, does not kill. It is the invisible radiation closely allied to the radiation of heat, which does the damage. In the main our atmosphere deflects this and other harmful radiations, but where it does get through human tissue suffers severely.

'What I am saying,' Quirke said deliberately, his blue eyes hard, 'is that K-74 exists in the sun in gaseous form, and in vast quantities, according to Rogers' observations. It is the radiation of this gaseous K-74 that strikes down many a living being on a summer's day. So then, K-74 reproduced in the laboratory and electrically heated behaves exactly as it does in the sun. It gradually volatilises, and as it does so the light becomes unbearable — as in the solar photosphere — and at the same time energy in the form of K-74 radiation is bound to be given off. And it is fatal! Deadly! It strikes straight to the brain of any living object and produces such terrific shock that syncope is the result. There, I think, we begin at last to grasp at the Satanic truth of this unholy business.'

'Yes,' Molly said slowly, musing over her coffee, 'but there is something that needs explaining, A.Q. The energy generated by an ordinary electric current cannot in any way be compared to the furious disintegrative atomic processes going on within the sun. So why is the effect the same at lower temperature? Or, more correctly, lower current power?'

'It simply means that K-74 volatilises at a fairly low temperature — as temperatures go. After all, if a metal volatilises at, say, three thousand Centigrade — which is the melting point of tungsten — it doesn't matter if you give it ten million Centigrade. It won't melt or volatilise any more on that account. K-74 volatilises at low temperature. It doesn't take solar power to make it break down. For instance, iron exists in the gaseous state in the sun, yet we too can make it into a gaseous state by temperatures inconceivably below those generated in the sun. Rogers obviously worked everything out and, offhand, I'd say the melting point of K-74 is around two thousand Centigrade. The present current power passed through our normal cables is about two thousand five hundred. That is an energy, and energy is only molecular action which the layman calls heat. So, then, during the process of reaching volatilising maximum, K-74 gives forth its substance in the form of unholy light, rising to lethal vibration, which ends in sudden extinction and ashes.'

'And that is what happened in the fatal lamp which killed De London?'

'I think so. Remember, we used a fair-sized lump of K-74. In the lamp design sketch I have seen a thin coating of K-74 is shown over the normal tungsten filament, Now, tungsten has to get a thousand degrees hotter than K-74 before it melts. So you see what happens? The current is switched on and the K-74 quickly lights up to apparent normal brilliance. Then it becomes rapidly super-brilliant — within a few seconds if there is only a thin coating. On again and the lethal radiation is blazed forth. Then extinction. All in a matter of perhaps three minutes from start to finish. The coating falls away in ash to the base of the globe and the normal tungsten filament goes on glowing in the usual way. And since heat is a negligible factor with K-74 the glass casing would not fuse or crack.'

6

Too many suspects

'It would seem,' Molly said at last, taking a deep breath, 'that you have the cause of death solved, A.Q. It was done by Rogers' deadly lamp, his son using the original idea and bringing it up to date as a modern lamp.'

Quirke was silent. Molly glanced at him.

'Boss, I said that . . . '

'Yes, yes, sweetheart, I heard you. Doubtless it is clear what kind of scientific method was employed, but was it young Rogers? Damn my doubts! Earlier I was sure of my ground . . . '

'He had ample motive.'

'Motive, yes. But had he the opportunity? You said earlier that perhaps old man Rogers sold his deadly lamp idea to De London. That's a distinct possibility, and maybe Rogers never got any financial return anyhow. But could young Rogers get at that lamp if it was in De London's strong room, as undoubtedly it would be? Rogers is a chauffeur-handyman and as such has no connection with the office itself. Again, how did Rogers put the lamp in the cube-room ceiling when it was twelve feet high and De London was right next to him, and guards outside?'

'He probably put the lamp in there some time before.'

'Not 'some time' before, Molly, otherwise the lamp might have worked before it was intended. It could have been put there on the day preceding the fatal night, yes, because there would be no particular reason to switch on the light. But certainly it could not have been put there any earlier. And Rogers, according to his daily movements, was not in the office during the daytime. The only time he came was a few minutes before De London locked himself in the cube-room. It's a knotty point, light of my life. Very knotty.'

'Harry de London, Owena, and Miss Turner would all be there during the day,'

Molly pointed out, then she frowned and shook her head. 'No they wouldn't. They only took over when the old man died — '

'Nevertheless, on the day of De London's death they visited him and they both went into the cube-room for a while. We have that on their own admission.'

Molly snapped her fingers. 'Maybe that's it! They did it between them! Yes, why not?' she went on eagerly. 'If Owena clambered on to Harry's shoulders — or even his arched back — she'd be able to reach the lamp. That does away with the need of any furniture!'

'Mmmm,' Quirke mused. 'Quite ingenious, but if we accept that fact we must also accept the fact that they knew all about the lamp. How did they ever discover it? Certainly not by entering De London's strong room or searching his files. Neither of them were connected with the De London business before the big fellow's death, so they'd have no opportunity. And anyway they'd both been away on Mars for a considerable time.'

'Then that leaves Miss Turner,' Molly said.

'Yes. Miss Turner.' Quirke considered for a moment. 'I am just thinking of something she said in conversation — to the effect that De London deprived her of the joys of youth and, in a sense, destroyed her. Logically, it is human nature when a person has destroyed you to try and destroy in return . . .'

Quirke struggled to his feet and stood breathing heavily, his eyes masked by profound inner thoughts. He actually gave a start when the visiphone shrilled. Molly went to it and switched on — to behold none other than Miss Turner herself in the scanning screen.

'Good morning, Miss Brayson,' she greeted formally. 'Might I have a word with Mr. Quirke?'

'Pleasure. He's here beside me.'

Quirke heaved himself across and picked up the instrument.

'Oh, Mr. Quirke, I've just thought of something which I felt you might like to know — concerning my employer's death, I mean.'

'Yes?' Quirke waited, his full moon face giving nothing away.

'I don't want to cast any undue suspicion upon Rogers, of course, but I think I ought to mention that the light installation for the foolproof room was his suggestion.'

'I see,' Quirke said, without moving a muscle.

'Originally,' Miss Turner hurried on, 'the foolproof room had no light at all. It was accidentally omitted, I believe, and Rogers noticed it. I know he suggested that lighting should be put in because I happened on him mentioning it to Mr. de London in the office one evening. Also, in case you don't know it already, the foolproof room was Rogers' own idea. He thought it the safest way for Mr. de London to avoid death in the manner threatened. Unhappily, it didn't work out.'

'Very kind of you to go out of your way to tell me this, Miss Turner,' Quirke commented. 'I assume you are alone in the office?'

'Of course — otherwise I wouldn't be

talking so freely. As I say, I don't wish to point a finger at Rogers any more than at anybody else, but when we're all under suspicion one has to do everything to try and establish the innocence or guilt of those concerned, don't you think?'

'Undoubtedly,' Quirke agreed gravely. 'Thank you so much, Miss Turner. I'm working hard on the case and every scrap of information is useful.'

Satisfied, Miss Turner rang off. Quirke stood thinking, his chubby lips compressed. Molly glanced at him.

'That almost seems to put Rogers back on the spot,' she said.

'Which may be the exact effect intended,' Quirke retorted.

'But you can't mean that Miss Turner — '

'Miss Turner could not know that our suspicions concerning Rogers have waned considerably; that I realise. But she might feel that the time I am taking to indict Rogers is indicative of my not being too sure of his guilt. Hence the extra information on her part to tilt the scale towards Rogers.'

'Look, boss, are you trying to say that Miss Turner is the guilty one?'

'I am facing an incontrovertible fact,' Quirke answered slowly. 'Namely, that Miss Turner was the only person with the opportunity! That is the point I've slipped up on so far. It is possible to pin a crime on anybody, but you have to think twice unless you can prove they had the opportunity to do it. Rogers, it seems, had no opportunity to get at the master-lamp because a commercial combine had it. We've assumed — and let's hope correctly — that De London was the person concerned. Right! Owena and Harry couldn't get at the lamp either. But Miss Turner could. A secretary in such a position of trust as she was could very easily get into the strong room. She probably knew the whole secret of the lamp. All she needed was the chance to use it in a convincing way . . . '

'But the cube-room wasn't her idea, boss. It was Rogers'. Again, if she had this lamp idea up her sleeve why didn't she use it earlier, in the office maybe?'

'Probably because she was never sure

whether De London would stay put long enough to get killed. In the cube-room she knew he wouldn't leave. It begins to look as though that cube-room proved the very chance she needed. As to opportunity in fixing the lamp — Well, I ask you! There were many times in the day before the fatal night when she could have had time to switch the cube lamps. Yes, it slowly begins to tie up.'

'And the induced nerves and the medicine? Does that tie up with doped cigars?'

'Certainly it does. There are cigars in the office — or rather were when De London was alive. Nothing simpler than to dope them. Again — opportunity! What makes me more certain than ever now that Miss Turner is mixed up in this is her sudden desire to hammer home this extra bit of information about Rogers. If she were perfectly innocent she'd probably leave me to find out all the odds and ends for myself.'

Molly reflected. Then: 'If she's the guilty party why on earth was she such a fool as to come to you for help because she wasn't satisfied with the circumstances of De London's death? He'd been put down and finished with. Why did she have to rake everything up again?'

'Vanity, m'dear. Vanity.'

Molly frowned. 'How d'you mean, A.Q.? What's vanity got to do with it?'

Puffing gently Quirke lumbered away from the visiphone and submerged in the nearest chair.

'Molly, in our time we've tackled quite a few criminal cases, and the outstanding point with every one of them is their colossal ego, their conviction that they can spit in the eye of the law. I see no reason to class Miss Turner as an exception. You see, to such people — especially those who work out what they believe is a foolproof crime — there is absolutely no point in having done it if nobody appreciates it. The whole great build-up just melts away into an anti-climax. Few ingenious killers can tolerate their handiwork being known only to themselves. You'll find that in looking down the crime archives. So then, convinced she had produced the perfect crime, Miss Turner decided to have an acknowledged expert view the result, feeling she was quite safe from detection — and just to make doubly sure it looks very much to me as though she did everything possible to deflect the blame to Rogers. Quite naturally, since every circumstance pointed in his direction . . . '

Quirke became silent for a while, debating his next move: then presently he nodded to himself.

'There is still the possibility that Miss Turner may be as innocent as anybody else,' he said, 'though I hardly think so. I need evidence, and to get it I'm going to Mars and root out who sent those messages. I'll get to the bottom of this business somehow.'

'Why,' Molly asked, 'did Miss Turner send messages to Rogers at the same time?'

'Possibly to heighten the suspicion against him, which to a certain degree it did.'

Molly sighed. 'To my mind, A.Q., Miss Turner is several kinds of a fool! She could have saved everything if she'd removed the lamp from the cube-room the following morning.'

'That was not possible. De London locked himself inside the cube-room and engineers had to blast the room open. After that the police and the guards were around. There was no chance whatever to switch lamps. And anyhow I don't think Miss Turner wanted to: she was so sure of herself with the existing lamp. Why not? It took me the devil of a time to find what was wrong with it.' Quirke lunged to his feet and coughed thickly. 'Anyway, light of my life, I'm heading for Mars on the next space-liner and you are going to stay behind and woo Miss Turner.'

'Huh?' Molly looked startled.

'I want you to find out, in that inimitable wheedling way which women have, just how much Miss Turner knows about the Rogers lamp. You can make it look as though your suspicions — and mine — rest upon Rogers. If she wonders where I am tell her I've been called away on urgent business.'

'Okay,' Molly sighed, 'but I'd much

rather come to Mars with you.'

'As the Burmese prophet once said, m'dear — no can do.' And Quirke quivered and wobbled immensely under the tides of merriment. As usual Molly took no notice. She picked up the empty coffee cups and took them over to the sink.

★   ★   ★

Quirke departed for Mars at eight o'clock that evening, and an hour later Molly Brayson kept a city restaurant appointment previously made with Miss Turner. From the willing way the De London secretary had agreed to the 'date' Molly wondered if Quirke was not perhaps riding the wrong horse after all.

'In case you're wondering where Mr. Quirke is,' Molly smiled, as she and Miss Turner settled at a corner table, 'he's away on urgent business.'

'Connected with the De London case?'

'That I don't know. He doesn't tell me everything . . . However, I do know the De London case is still uppermost in his mind and that is why we're here tonight . . . '

Molly paused and orders were given to the waiter. Then Miss Turner sat back in her chair — angular, cold, yet somehow vaguely eager.

'I hope Mr. Quirke is getting near to an arrest,' she said. 'It's not pleasant being under suspicion and the papers and newscasts are beginning to point the finger, too. Mr. de London's death from foul play is exciting enormous interest.'

'I'm aware of it.' Molly held forth cigarettes, which Miss Turner declined. 'Which makes me wonder, Miss Turner, why you dragged this business into the daylight when everything was more or less settled.'

'I did it purely because I couldn't swallow the coincidence of the notes sent to Mr. de London, and the synchronised fashion in which he met his death. The thing was too obvious. It had to be murder — brilliantly arranged.'

'Mr. Quirke,' Molly said slowly, 'is working on the theory that De London died through the influence of a most unusual electric lamp, the one which we removed during the investigation.'

'Oh?' Miss Turner's eyebrows rose. 'Surely that is rather a waste of time? An electric lamp couldn't kill.'

'Not a normal one, true. The one we have is not normal. It is lethal — or was to commence with. Our only problem now is to decide who had access to it. To the best of our belief it was in De London's possession to begin with, and originally invented by Henry Rogers.'

'Ah! You mean you are building the case against Rogers the chauffeur?'

'Naturally,' Molly smiled, and waited as the waiter laid out the refreshment. 'What other conclusion is there? Rogers must have cashed in on his father's invention — but what I have to learn from you, on behalf of Mr. Quirke is whether such an invention was even in the De London files.'

'A lethal electric lamp?' Miss Turner sipped at her drink for a long time and Molly watched her covertly, drawing at her cigarette and apparently pondering deep issues.

'I suppose it was in Henry Rogers' lifetime?' Miss Turner asked suddenly.

'Naturally, since he invented it.'

'How can Mr. Quirke be so sure that Henry Rogers did invent it?'

'He is, and he has incontestable proof. Something to do with the age of the ink on the formula, or something. Rogers invented it all right. We have copies of his original plans.'

'And what was supposed to happen then?'

'We believe the lamp was handed over to De London as a weapon of war, to be used against invaders as a sneak killer. We want proof that such a lamp was given to De London, and we must also know whether Rogers could have had access to it.'

Here, Molly felt convinced, Miss Turner would seize the supreme opportunity to blacken the younger Rogers to the limit, but to her amazement the opposite happened.

'I've never heard of such a lamp, Miss Brayson. And even if there were one Rogers would never be able to get at it. To do that he'd have to either get past me, or the night guard, and there is no record of him having attempted either.'

Molly took a sip of her own drink, somewhat puzzled as to what to do next. The whole 'wheedling process' had gone off the rails somewhere.

'It would seem, then, that such a lamp was not bought by De London, but by somebody else,' she said at last.

'Very unlikely!' Miss Turner declared dogmatically, and Molly gave her a surprised glance.

'Why unlikely?'

'Because everything which Henry Rogers ever invented was sold by contractual obligation to De London. Some fifteen years ago I recall making out that contract under Mr. de London's direction. It called for first option on everything Henry Rogers invented, and I am prepared to swear that no lethal lamp was ever offered. It is not for me to cast reflections on my late employer's business methods,' Miss Turner added, 'but I will say that Henry Rogers never received the considerable monies to which he was entitled. He considered Henry Rogers as a genius just asking to be plucked — and plucked he was. Which is why I think the son may be responsible for everything, getting his own back for the way his father was treated.'

'Yes — probably,' Molly admitted, feeling completely out of her depth.

'There are so many angles,' Miss Turner sighed. 'As I said to Mr. Quirke, I don't want to point suspicion more at one person than another, so I suppose, if it comes to that, Mr. de London junior and his wife are also targets.'

'Have you any personal reaction towards them?' Molly asked.

'Not particularly. I work well enough with them, though I do rather object to Mrs. de London — Owena, I mean — taking the reins so constantly out of her husband's hands. I hardly know from which one I am supposed to take orders. I do believe that before very long Owena de London will become the governing director of the organisation and push her husband right out of it. She's a brilliant businesswoman, extremely ambitious, and anything but the quiet, simple young woman she made herself appear at first. I have been quite disagreeably surprised. I suppose though, that I shouldn't be. She is of high Martian rank and extremely intelligent, and if she could wed the gigantic De London interests to the great combines of the Martian Nardins, controlled by her Martian mother, it would be a conquest indeed.'

'You think that may be her aim?' Molly asked slowly.

'Now De London senior is out of the way, yes . . . If I had her intelligence I'd probably do the same thing myself.'

★　★　★

Meantime, several million miles from Earth Adam Quirke's titanic bulk was sprawled in one of the armchairs of the space liner's 'solarium'. Quirke was apparently at peace with all men — a cooling drink at his side, a 3-D projected orchestra playing a lulling refrain, and outside the giant bowed windows loomed the void. Then Quirke's peace was interrupted by the presence of a page at his side.

'Radiophone call from Earth, Mr. Quirke — a Miss Brayson. Will you take it here?'

Quirke nodded, and took the instrument as it was handed to him.

'Well, light of my life?' he asked sleepily, and after an interval Molly's voice floated over the millions of miles of void.

'I've just come back from my interview with Miss Turner boss. She's got me all mixed up, or else she's confoundedly clever. I don't know what to think.'

'Let me do the thinking, love, and you just talk,' Quirke replied at length. 'Word for word, what happened?' Quirke waited for the reply, which came after a short interval. In detail Molly recounted the conversation as near as she could remember it.

'After which,' she finished, 'things sort of fell flat. I thanked her for what she'd told me and we parted on the best of terms. Honest, A.Q., I can't somehow see her as the killer. Not now. She had so many wonderful chances to blacken Rogers and she didn't take them. No woman could be that smart.'

A further pause whilst the radio waves crossed the gulf of space. Quirke's blue eyes were narrowed but his voice was honey itself when he answered:

'You've done your best, light of my life, and no gal could do more. Take a vacation until I return. God knows you've earned it. If during that vacation you run into anything unusual just buzz me.' A pause, then:

'Right, boss — and thanks. I'll miss you.'

Quirke boomed and rumbled over some obscure joke concerning the wonder of anybody missing his size; then he becalmed abruptly and sat in fathoms' deep concentration, the 'phone clutched in his hand until the page came and politely removed it.

'Thanks, laddie,' Quirke muttered, handing over a tip. 'I was right out beyond the ken of things.'

'Yessir,' the boy muttered, and went on his way wondering if the white-haired

Buddha was an old-time actor of some sort.

And in a matter of seconds Quirke had relapsed again. He had the singular gift, shared with very few people of utterly detaching himself from his surroundings and living entirely within his mind. In this way he could pursue any line of reasoning to either a logical or illogical conclusion. And so it was now. The only movement he made was to put down a note in case a point escaped him. His final note read:

'The Nardins of Mars, the highest caste — direct descendants of the original scientist colonists — and the mightiest commercial enterprise on the red planet, of which Owena is a member. More, she is the only daughter of the highest Nardin of all. The love of Owena for Harry de London is no longer marked by girlish and clinging affection, but by domination absolute. There arises the great question: was Gyron de London right when he viewed Owena with such rank disfavour? Had he more behind his animosity than mere resentment at the wedding of Martian and Terranian?'

'Interesting,' Quirke murmured, viewing what he had written, 'extremely interesting. The twist and the turns, the brilliant red herrings, the ingenuity, the flawless preparation. But then, if one deals with an advanced mind — such as anybody with a part Martian upbringing must have — one must expect fireworks. The point is: can A.Q. douse those fireworks completely?'

He smiled to himself, put his notes away, then got to his feet and retired to his suite.

For the rest of the journey to Mars he appeared quite detached from all problems, spending most of the time resting his colossal bulk — but the moment Mars was reached he was as active as ever. His first call after being given clearance by the spaceport customs and medicos was upon the police authorities in Duo City, the metropolis roughly divided into half-Earth and half-Martian communities, a city standing close to the edge of one of Mars' relentless deserts.

The chief of the police authorities was

Douglas Anzia, a half-Martian, half-Earth man. Not that this in any way detracted from his cordiality and high standing.

'Delighted, Mr. Quirke,' he said, shaking hands. 'Long time since you had reason to come to Mars.'

'And I wouldn't be here now except for urgent business,' A.Q. responded, sitting down heavily. 'As I explained to you in my advance radiogram, I'm working on the De London case and need to make a thorough check of the mails to Earth from about the first of March onwards. Did you manage to do anything for me in that direction?'

'I did yes, as far as possible, and there is a complete list of mails sent to Earth. Here it is.'

The chief of police handed it across and Quirke studied it. Then he nodded.

'Four of them to Gyron de London. That's correct — tallying with the two he received and the two sent to Rogers, his handyman-chauffeur. Did you get any clue as to who sent these?'

'In the normal way it would have been next to impossible — as difficult as you on Earth having to detect one particular person having sent one particular letter — and not registering or insuring it, either. In this case, though, the matter was simplified because the mail-collector remembers where these letters came from. A private mail-collection box.'

'You mean one of the boxes belonging to the governing body of this planet?'

'Yes. The Controlesque.'

'One final guess,' Quirke mused. 'It was one of the boxes — or maybe the only box — used by the Nardin family, who are high-ranking members of the Controlesque, or governing Martian body.'

The chief of police gave a rather whimsical smile. 'It would seem, Mr. Quirke, that you have the facts without our needing to help you.'

'The verification was what I needed — and now I have it. When I began my journey to Mars I had no preconceived ideas concerning the Controlesque, but I have now — thanks to a very diligent secretary back on Earth. I am not concerned with the Controlesque as a whole, but with the Nardins in particular. I thank you, Chief, for your valuable information.'

Quirke struggled to his feet, shook hands, and went on his way. As he went he looked interestedly about him. It was difficult to realize that he was on an alien world. Far overhead was the impenetrable protective dome that covered the entire city and kept in the Earth-normal atmosphere. It also filtered out the intense cosmic and ultra-violet radiation that fell on the Martian desert plain outside, whilst allowing the weak sunlight to get through. Strategically placed public lighting gave the effect of daylight. Buried in the ground beneath his feet, he knew, were artificial gravity generators that boosted the weaker Martian gravity to Earth-normal. Outside the dome Mars was a hostile and dead world.

Ten minutes walk brought him to the mightiest edifice in Duo City, the great building which housed the administrative and living quarters of the Martian government. One side of the building was devoted to business and the other to private apartments. On the long bronze-gold plate that Quirke studied were the names of the high-rank Martian families who constituted all that was supreme in Martian business and society.

Eventually he arrived at 'Nardin: Apartment 7, 8th Floor'. He went into the building's enormous hall, took the self-service elevator, and was quickly whisked to the middle reaches of the building.

A Martian-born servant opened the apartment door to him.

'Adam Quirke soliciting an audience with Ianta Nardin,' Quirke explained, handing over his card. 'It is most urgent and concerns her daughter Owena.'

'Will you be so good as to step inside, Mr. Quirke?'

7

Quirke trumps a murderer

Quirke lumbered into the huge reception room and seated himself, his eyes passing over the spotless furniture, the dozen and one scientific gadgets to make life easier and more entertaining, and finally to the great windows through which the shrunken sun was pallidly shining. Then the door of the inner apartment clicked and a tall, gracious-looking woman of advancing years came into view. Her clothes were vivid in colouring and clung to her still slender figure with the softness of golden silk. Here was Ianta Nardin, born of Martian parents, and a leading member of the Martian nobility.

'How are you, Mr. Quirke . . . ' She shook hands gently as Quirke surged to his feet. 'This is the first time I have had the pleasure of a personal meeting, though, of course, your name is quite familiar to me.'

'You are more than gracious to acknowledge the fact.'

Quirke murmured, inclining his head with its mop of unruly white hair.

The uncrowned queen of Mars seated herself with easy grace and Quirke settled back again in his chair. The extraordinary eyes of the woman of Mars pinned him.

'Now, Mr. Quirke, what brings you here?'

'I am afraid,' Quirke replied gravely, 'that my mission is not a pleasant one, but because the Nardins of Mars are no ordinary people I felt it my duty to acquaint you with certain facts . . . I am afraid that you are unlikely to see your daughter Owena again.'

'What!' Ianta Nardin gave a start and her eyes widened. 'But why not? Has something happened to her? Why do you have to tell me this? Why not her husband — '

Quirke raised his podgy hand slowly. 'A moment, madam, if you please. Let me explain. Since my name is familiar to you,

you will also be aware that my profession is that of a scientific investigator — '

'Yes, yes. I know. But what — '

'I am directly concerned with finding the right answer to the death of Gyron de London, one of Earth's greatest commercial giants. He was murdered.'

'So I heard.' Ianta Nardin looked troubled. 'But, Mr. Quirke, what has this to do with my daughter?'

'Everything. Your daughter was the killer.'

'Mr. Quirke!' The Martian woman rose with dignity to her feet. 'Whilst I respect your famous name and ability, I must protest against — '

'Protest, madam, is pointless.' Quirke had also risen, his round face grim, his voice determined. 'I have spent a very long time working out this problem and every factor now points straight to your daughter. I shall not bother you with the details. I merely warn you that after your daughter has been arrested by Earth law — as she will be — you will not see her again.'

A speechless look of anguish crossed

Ianta Nardin's face. Quirke waited, his blue eyes fixed on her.

'How — how can you be sure of such a ghastly fact?' she asked at last, faltering.

'That, madam, is my business — with all respect. You are not involved in this, therefore — '

'But I am involved in it!' Ianta Nardin stopped dead, her lower lip between her white teeth. It looked as though she could have bitten out her tongue for having said that one line.

'Thank you, madam, for the observation,' Quirke murmured. 'Would you perhaps care to enlarge upon it?'

'If it will do anything to save Owena, yes. Anything, Mr. Quirke, to prevent the ultimate disgrace descending upon us!'

'The law will take no cognizance of rank or standing, madam, but if you have something which may — er — ameliorate things then I am prepared to listen.'

He waited until the Martian woman had reseated herself, then once more he squeezed into the nearby big chair and puffed heavily. In courteous silence he waited for the woman to get a hold over her emotions.

'Owena acted under my orders,' she said at last, averting her face.

'That does not absolve her from blame, madam. She is a grown woman and knows the difference between right and wrong. Had she not wished to commit murder no power of your devising could have made her.'

'I did not say she wasn't willing. She was! And why? Because of the withering scorn in which Gyron de London held her. She hated him more than any man on Earth. She would have given up the idea of marrying Harry de London had I not pointed out that that was just what Gyron de London wanted her to do. So she married — no longer for love — for she could not love a De London any more after the way Gyron de London had behaved — but to achieve a purpose. My purpose!'

'Your purpose being, I think, to wed the vast commercial interests of the De London organisation to the Controlesque of Mars? A merger of interplanetary interests which would never have been possible whilst De London lived?'

'Yes.' The Martian woman's voice was still quiet; then she suddenly looked up, her clenched fists giving the clue to her emotion. 'Understand this, Mr. Quirke: my daughter acted as she did because I ordered her to, not as her mother but as one of the ruling factions of this planet. She dared not disobey.'

Quirke smiled faintly. 'That does not convince me, madam. The dictates of one's own conscience are far more powerful than the orders of a near-ruler, such as you are. Your daughter's act stands self-condemned. As I see it she murdered De London because she, as much as you, wanted to see the merging of Earth and Martian interests, with strong bias on the Martian side. She also wanted personal revenge on De London. Both very strong motives. But she did not want to be found out so, before she committed the act, she made certain plans to deflect the blame from herself.'

'Yes,' Ianta looked at Quirke thoughtfully. 'You say you have proof of everything she has done?'

'I now have proof that she did commit the murder. I hadn't until you started explaining.'

'But you said — '

'I am sorry for the deception, madam. I'm something of a psychologist and, knowing Owena would protect herself if I made an effort to question her, I decided to tackle you. It struck me as reasonable that, as her mother, you would do your utmost to tell the whole story, even blacken your own side of the case, just as long as your child was shielded from the wrath to come. I guessed right. You have explained facts which I had already formulated.'

'You are a clever man, Mr. Quirke.'

'A resourceful one, madam. But the story is not yet told. There is much your daughter did. Let me suggest to you what happened: Through Harry de London she had the chance of discovering the identities of those most closely connected with De London in his business life — such as Henry Rogers, the inventor, his son who became De London's chauffeur, Miss Turner, the faithful secretary — and she doubtless discovered that Miss Turner and young Rogers both had ample reason for wanting to be rid of De London.'

'Yes, she found that out — and reported to me.'

'She also found out, probably, that Henry Rogers, when alive, was under contract to De London to hand him all his inventions?'

'Yes. That information came from the younger Rogers himself. Owena purposely made a friend of him in the few times she saw him on her Earth visits prior to the marriage.'

'And out of this information concerning Rogers she devised a clever scientific plot, specially designed to throw guilt on Rogers, or — more remotely — upon secretary Turner.'

Ianta Nardin was silent, but there was a faint colour in her normally pale cheeks.

'You people of Mars are clever scientists,' Quirke continued, 'and for that reason the exact science of death by radiation would probably be child's play. I was led astray by giving to Henry Rogers the credit for possessing more scientific genius than he really had. I was led to think — as was intended — that he devised a lethal lamp for defence purposes and gave it to De London. It was Miss Turner who exploded this theory to my own secretary, for there is no record of any such invention ever having been handed in by Henry Rogers. Your daughter, I imagine, was clever enough to discover the whereabouts of the Rogers laboratory and put therein plans and notes relating to a lethal lamp in the hope the younger Rogers — if investigation got that far — would be involved. She had evidently learned that he rarely used the laboratory, therefore there was little chance of him discovering the foisted plans — and even if he had done so he would have accepted them as his father's. Even apparent age in the ink and papers was cleverly faked, a not very difficult matter with science such as yours . . . '

'You are entirely correct,' Ianta Nardin

said, a tautness about her mouth which seemed to indicate she was thinking swiftly.

'As to the rest . . . ' Quirke's huge shoulders rose and fell. 'Your daughter had merely to have a lamp made in laboratories here and take it with her to Earth — probably when she returned from the honeymoon with Harry de London. The simple matter of altering the lamp into an apparently modern one would present no trouble to her technical skill. She sent letters of warning in advance to confuse the issue and scare De London, sending similar notes to Rogers to throw guilt on to him. There were other things she did — such as drugging cigars, or else switching normal cigars for the same brand in a drugged variety. Her opportunity was there for she was right inside the De London home after the honeymoon when De London first began to get attacks of nerves. It can and does fit in madam, but there are still loose ends which your daughter will be compelled to explain for herself.'

'Such as?' Ianta Nardin asked.

'She did not know, I think, that a

cube-room would be devised for De London's 'safety', so I am left to the assumption that her original intention was to use the lethal lamp in some other way — until the cube-room presented a more spectacular opportunity.'

'Her original intention. Mr. Quirke, until she was ordered out of the De London house along with her husband, was to put the lamp in De London's desklight. Every evening he spent a certain time there and that would have been as efficient as the cube-room method. She used the cube-room because, to make the warning come true, it was all she could do. The deterrent was that she could not move the lamp afterwards. She trusted to the secret not being found — and unfortunately underestimated your powers.'

'There is still one final point,' Quirke said. 'When did she have the opportunity to fit the lamp in place? I think my secretary gave me the answer to that and I told her not to be ridiculous.'

'I cannot answer that question, Mr. Quirke, because Owena has not told me the exact details, but in every fact leading up to the disposal of De London you are uncannily correct. I would add that I do not regret wiping out De London. He stood for everything that was arrogant and brutal. Interplanetary trade was strangled by his iron hold. He was only concerned with his own advancement and the fact that he was damming the normal circulation of business did not concern him one jot.'

'Nevertheless, madam, he was a man and a citizen — and therefore the one who terminated his life must stand trial for murder. You yourself will also be involved as an accessory.'

'Perhaps,' the Martian woman answered, with a strange smile. Then she rose majestically to her feet. 'I have nothing further to add, Mr. Quirke. You must act as you see fit — but I hope my frankness will have helped the position somewhat against my daughter.'

Quirke struggled up and inclined his head. 'I will do my best, madam — and thank you.'

He left the apartment quietly and the

manservant closed the door upon him. Still in the apartment reception lounge Ianta opened the front of what appeared to be one of her many jewel-studded bracelets. Adjusting the tiny button on its top she spoke quietly.

'I'm alone now. Did you hear all that, Owena?' Her message sent, Ianta poured herself a drink and settled down on a divan to wait for the reply. After nearly eight minutes had elapsed — the time taken for radio waves to cross the 40-million mile gap to Earth and back — the reply came.

'I heard it, mother.' The voice was remote but audible. 'I never thought a private radio waveband could come in so useful. You think of everything. You needn't worry. I'll deal with Mr. Quirke — effectively.'

Ianta smiled. 'I thought you would, my dear. You are so resourceful.'

★ ★ ★

His Martian business concluded, Quirke wasted no time in returning to Earth, informing Molly Brayson by interplanetary radio of the success of his Martian mission — but somewhat to Quirke's surprise Molly did not answer. Which was most unusual for her. She had never before failed to acknowledge a communication from her boss when it had been sent her.

'There's one possible answer to this,' Quirke told himself, as the space liner touched down at the London spaceport, 'and I hope I've guessed wrong.'

He had not. He discovered that when he arrived at his home and laboratory. Neither the housekeeper nor Molly Brayson were present — but Owena de London was. Quirke discovered her in the laboratory, entirely at her ease, a deceptive smile on her good-looking face.

'Hello Mr. Quirke!' she greeted him pleasantly enough and rose from her chair. 'Well equipped laboratory you have here — and plenty of food and comforts too. I've been quite happy whilst waiting for you to return home.'

Quirke looked her up and down, his blue eyes hard. 'Which means, I suppose, that you know all the details of my interview with your mother?'

'I do, yes. Mother and I have a private radio waveband, the pick-up being on our wrists. When either of us have anything important we wish overheard we simply signal with the invaluable little instrument — which looks no bigger than a wristwatch, but is immensely powerful — and there you are.'

'With your permission,' Quirke said, 'I'll sit. I'm too heavy a man to stand about for long.'

'Yes, do. Make yourself comfortable.' Owena also sat, choosing the nearest upright chair. Then her large-pupilled eyes roved over Quirke's monstrous form as he reclined.

'I suppose the disappearance of my secretary and housekeeper is your doing, Owena?'

'Of course. Fortunately I didn't have to trouble over your wife as she is visiting relatives in Europe. Yes, Mr. Quirke, I know everything you told my mother, and I must congratulate you upon your sagacity. The extra little bit that worries you — as to how I changed the lamp in the cube-room — can easily be explained. My husband bent down so that I could use his back as a 'chair'. Nothing could have been easier.'

'Exactly what my secretary thought,' Quirke mused. 'From which I gather your husband knows all about your activities?'

'Not a thing. Though he had no love for his father he would certainly never have agreed to connive in murdering him. No, to get him to bend his back I merely said that the shade around the lamp looked as though it were falling off. Since Harry, in his stooped position, could not see what I was doing he never suspected a thing. He's a dear boy, Mr. Quirke, but not very bright.'

'Compared to you I can well credit that. But come to the point, Owena. Obviously this isn't a social call you're making. What are your terms?'

'I imagine,' Owena said, thinking, 'that you consider the lives of your house-keeper and Miss Brayson are worth saving, so I am willing to return them both to you in return for your dropping the case against me and my mother. Tell the world you can't find the answer and everything will be well.'

'By which statement you reveal you are still very young,' Quirke murmured. 'Even if the lives of my housekeeper and Molly Brayson should be forfeited, I still would not allow you to escape the penalty due for your crime.'

Owena sighed. 'I was afraid you'd say that — and after all the trouble I took to have those two abducted and hidden away! Very well then, since the merging of Martian and Earthly business interests cannot now be disturbed there's only one answer. You will have to be disposed of, Mr. Quirke. My mother and I cannot allow our plans, which have come to maturity, to be blown sky-high just because you have hide-bound conceptions about murder and the penalty due therefore. On Mars we rid ourselves of those who block progress or are unwanted and — '

'This is Earth, Owena, not Mars, and I shall carry out my duty as far as I possibly can. Killing me won't avail you anything, you know.'

'I think it will. It will dispose of the only person who knows the facts.'

Quirke shook his mane of white hair. 'On the contrary, Owena. You are now in a laboratory which contains a hundred and one scientific instruments, together with a variety of hidden switches — and I am the only living person who knows where the switches are and what purpose they serve. It will interest you to know that at this very moment this whole laboratory, and you and myself, are being televised into police headquarters, together with a radio reproduction of our conversation. So you see, even if I die the police know the facts, and you will be hounded down no matter where you may go.'

Owena looked sharply about her. 'I don't see any switches! Most certainly I haven't seen you move one since you came in here.'

'You have overlooked the usual qualities of intercepting a photo-electric cell.' Quirke gave a grim smile. 'I am never alone in this laboratory unless I really wish to be.'

'Bluff!' Owena shouted, striding forward. 'Sheer bluff!'

'I assure you it is not. If you kill me your act will be visible to those who are watching at Scotland Yard. In fact it is more than probable that a squad of men are heading here at this very moment!'

That Owena was unsure of herself was more than obvious. In words she had already given herself away, and admitted abducting two innocent citizens. If she was televised in the act of murdering Quirke she would be picked up within an hour, no matter how much she tried to escape. Then suddenly an idea seemed to strike her. She swung away and headed for a corner of the laboratory where the main generators were humming musically. Seizing the massive power switch that governed them she pulled it over to zero.

'If your television is still working I'll be surprised!' she declared, swinging round again. 'How do you like — '

She stopped. In the brief seconds that

had elapsed Quirke had risen from his chair and was standing right beside her, a hypodermic syringe in his hand with plunger extended. Before Owena had a chance to grasp what had happened Quirke seized her in a grip that held her immovable; then she felt the sharp stab of the needle as it sank into her arm.

'I dislike rough treatment but sometimes it is necessary,' Quirke said, breathing heavily. 'I have injected a virulent poison into your bloodstream, Owena. In five minutes you will drop dead unless the antidote is used. I am prepared to use it if you tell me where my secretary and housekeeper are.'

Owena glared at him furiously and in those few seconds the veneer of Earth culture vanished. That she was more Martian than Terran at heart was plain.

'I'm dictating the terms — not you!' she shouted in fury.

Quirke did not answer. He glanced up at the clock. Owena glanced too and then thrust her hand into the pocket of her costume jacket. Instantly Quirke seized her arm and forced her to withdraw the hand quickly.

'I could very easily pin you at the point of a gun,' he said, 'but I do not think it necessary. I am so much bigger than you,' he added dryly.

Owena relaxed, trembling a little. The clock finger moved remorselessly onwards and Quirke waited. Finally the fight seemed to go out of the half-Martian girl.

'All right,' she muttered. 'They're in one of the basements at the De London residence. My husband doesn't know since he was at the office when I had the abduction made.'

'Thank you. And you freely admit you murdered Gyron de London in the manner I described to your mother?'

'Yes, yes, I admit it. For God's sake hurry with that antidote! The five minutes are nearly up.'

'Water,' Quirke grinned, 'does not require an antidote. That was all I injected into you, Owena. Aqua pura!'

'What!'

'As for my television and radio — just a little game of bluff even as you suggested. I rather thought you might forget yourself

— and me — for the moment and seek a means of killing the power in this laboratory. That gave me a chance to move, to good advantage. I will admit that our conversation, from the moment when I injected you, has been transmitted to the police. I moved the necessary switch when your back was turned. So there are many witnesses to your admission that you murdered De London.'

Owena was silent, massaging her arm gently from where the needle had stabbed her. Quirke waited for a moment and then lumbered to the laboratory door, opening it.

'After you,' he said, quietly. 'We have an appointment with the Police Commissioner.'

We do hope that you have enjoyed reading this large print book.

Did you know that all of our titles are available for purchase?

We publish a wide range of high quality large print books including:
Romances, Mysteries, Classics
General Fiction
Non Fiction and Westerns

Special interest titles available in large print are:
The Little Oxford Dictionary
Music Book, Song Book
Hymn Book, Service Book

Also available from us courtesy of Oxford University Press:
Young Readers' Dictionary
(large print edition)
Young Readers' Thesaurus
(large print edition)

For further information or a free brochure, please contact us at:
Ulverscroft Large Print Books Ltd.,
The Green, Bradgate Road, Anstey,
Leicester, LE7 7FU, England.
Tel: (00 44) **0116 236 4325**
Fax: (00 44) **0116 234 0205**

Other titles in the
Linford Mystery Library:

THE CLEOPATRA SYNDICATE

Sydney J. Bounds

Maurice Cole, the inventor of a mysterious new perfume, is found murdered. But his employer's only concern is to recover the stolen perfume . . . He hires Daniel Shield, head of I.C.E. — the Industrial Counter Espionage agency — who is aided by Barney Ryker and the beautiful Melody Gay. The trail leads them to Egypt, where Shield must find international criminal Suliman Kalif and recover the perfume before the Nile runs red with the blood of a Holy War.